Companion Volume to the Star Trails Tetralogy

The Star Trails Compendium

Terms, Definitions, Weather, Political Structure, and Planetary Description of the Cyrarian Planetary System

Compiled by

Marcha Fox

Kalliope Rising Press
Burnet, Texas

This is a work of fiction created to accompany the novels in the Star Trails Tetralogy series. While some of the information contained herein such as scientific terminology is accurate, much of it is fictitious and only intended to clarify places, technologies and situations referred to in the stories. Many are products of the author's imagination or used fictitiously and are not to be construed as real. Any resemblance to actual events, locales or entities living or dead is entirely coincidental.

Kalliope Rising Press
P.O. Box 23
Burnet, Texas 78611

http://www.StarTrailsSaga.com

First Printing May 2015
Expanded and Revised July 2015
Printed in U.S.A.

Cover design, interior design and illustrations by the author

ISBN-10:0988333554
ISBN-13:978-0988333550

Star Trails Tetralogy
by Marcha Fox

Beyond the Hidden Sky
A Dark of Endless Days
A Psilent Place Below
Refractions of Frozen Time

NOTES

TABLE OF CONTENTS

STAR TRAILS TERMS AND DEFINITIONS

A

Aborra: A private area where a person could keep their personal possessions and have some degree of privacy. It sometimes but not always included a sleeping cyll.

Acceleration Shell: A gel-filled inflatable shield that absorbs extreme accelerations incident to space travel which is similar to the effects of being submerged in a tank of water.

Advanced Life Support and Intervention Center (ALSIC): Similar to a modern Earth hospital but with more advanced technologies.

Aerogel: Extremely light substance used for insulation as well as a medium used in space experiments to capture cosmic dust or particles moving at an extremely high velocity.

Ahir Budhyana: A Vedic mythological god associated with water and darkness and stands for the combination of consciousness with eternity. It can also represent wisdom in the form of a snake. This deity is honored on Earth as well in India where it is part of the Vedic tradition.

Algon, Algonian: Fictitious star-system located in the fourth quadrant of the Sagittarius Arm of the Hostii (Milky Way) galaxy and location of the planet, Verdaris.

Algorithm: A specific procedure for calculating a certain result either in math or computer programming.

Anachorda Corridor: Fictitious area of the galaxy between two blackholes and various other objects with a lot of gravity which compress space and time naturally, creating the same effect as a starship's third harmonic warp drive which compresses distance by a ratio of a thousand to one. A very dangerous route for inexperienced spacers, however, due to inherent instabilities.

Angular Velocity: Speed typically measured in degrees of an object rotating around a central axis such as a planet.

Anoia: Fictitious sport on Mira III which has similarities to baseball, basketball and soccer.

Antimatter Annihilation: The process which occurs when matter and antimatter connect and destroy each other.

APU: See Auxiliary Power Unit

Aquifer: Water deposit or underground river contained within layers of rock.

Arcturian: Fictitious, highly intelligent being from the star-system, Arcturus that has the appearance of a human-sized ant. They communicate using telepathy and require everyone to agree (consensus) before taking action.

Asylum: Giving a person such as one accused of a crime a safe place to stay, such as someone leaving a hostile country and going to one where they will be treated fairly.

Asystolic: Medical condition when a person's heart stops beating, i.e. cardiac arrest.

Automaton: Fictitious term for a robotic device designed for a specific task. Appearance is that of a machine as opposed to human.

Auxiliary Power Unit (APU): Unit similar to a battery used to generate electricity and thus power a space craft.

Avionics: Electronics related to the operation of aviation and space vehicles.

B

Ballome: Portable structures formed from inflatable epoxy that cures and hardens in the ultraviolet rays of the sun. Used for temporary outposts on primitive worlds. Most contain basic heating and cooling systems and gel insulation that protects from most climates as well as plumbing. Usually have a galley kitchen, living area and two bedrooms equipped with built-in sleeping cylls.

Benefics: The positive energy inherent in the Universe which can be manifested through good deeds and thoughts. In areas where it predominates it can provide metaphysical assistance to mankind.

Bezarna: Fictitious blackhole used as a galactic prison from which no one can escape.

Biometrics: Electronic recognition of an individual based on facial recognition technology.

Blackhole: What is left of a massive star's core after its life ends. Relatively small yet extremely dense and heavy, their gravity is so strong that even light cannot escape.

Bnolar: A telepathic cave-dwelling species indigenous to Cyraria. They measure over two meters tall when fully erect, supported by two heavy back legs and a long, heavy tail for balance (similar to a kangaroo). They have six arms and scooplike paws with three heavy claws which enable them to dig through dirt extremely fast. Multi-layered skin is irridescent so it reflects heat as well as detached from muscle tissue giving it a cloak-like in appearance. Their deepset eyes are veiled by skin layers when exposed to sunlight but appear as silver orbs when inside their caverns.

Bondling: Legal mate or spouse bound to another person through a ceremony performed by the Ledorian Order.

Bowl Bush: Fictitious plant native to Cyraria with flowers which resemble a large bowl and a large, bulbous edible root.

Brain, Left or Right: The brain is divided down the middle into two obvious sides which are referred to as the right and left hemispheres. The right hemisphere tends to be more creative and intuitive and the left hemisphere more logical. Most people use one side more than the other while some do well using both.

Brazoboro: Fictitious tree native to the planet, Verdaris with branches which have ring-like groupings of needle-like leaves similar to Earth's pine trees.

C

Calmanac: Combination calendar, almanac and ephemeris used on Cyraria to track the seasons, temperature, dust and ultraviolet radiation levels, position of the dual suns, which are visible and for how long, and the probability of storms and ground quakes.

Capacitance: The amount of electrical charge stored in a device known as a capacitor.

Cavern: Underground cave formed either by rain dripping through limestone and dissolving it or an underground river.

=CC=: Cyrarian Credit used as money on Cyraria.

C-com: Common term for a fictitious device known formally as a Cerebral Companion. Similar to Earth's "smart phones" in its ability to access information, it also can store a person's thoughts and knowledge which is downloaded and accessed telepathically. An extension of a person's brain to which it is linked through a cell-mate quantum link. Its advanced capabilities utilize artificial intelligence which greatly augments its user's abilities.

Cellulated Botonics: Fictitious term for cloned wood fiber used for construction on worlds where trees are rare or don't exist and there are no other suitable building materials.

Centripetal Force: A force from the center, such as that imposed by a string attached to a rotating ball. Note that this is different from centrifugal force, the pseudo-force which is a form of inertia such as that generated by a centrifuge. Another example is when you feel as if you're pushed to the side opposite the direction in which a vehicle is turning as your body wants to continue moving the way it was going.

Chimera padre: Literally means the genes inherited from the father but also used to refer to one's father. Usually shortened to 'merapa, similar to the casual Earth term, dad.

Chron: Time measurement used when there is no visible sun or other means for observing the passage of time. Space term used to designate a day but consists of 26 Earth hours instead of the usual 24.

Chronometer: Time measurement device similar to a clock or watch.

Chronoviatic: Fictitious term for the ability to facilitate time travel.

Code 60: Fictitious term used as a warning or to designate an extreme emergency.

Code Orange: Tenth level of the Miran Academic system which is identified by wearing an orange uniform. Each level has its own color for easy identification.

Comcenter: Communication center where messages can be sent or received.

Comcon: Communications console or terminal similar to a computer monitor except most project a holographic image into the air rather than being confined to a screen.

Concurrency Reviews: Cyrarian equivalent of news broadcasts or podcasts.

Countermeasures: Actions taken to prevent something adverse from occurring.

Cristobalite: Fictitious variety of crystal found in Cyrarian caverns. Their properties are unique, valuable and capable of transmitting thought (psi) waves and channeling information, i.e. cristoviatic properties.

Cristoviatic: Fictitious term for the ability to transmit psi waves.

Cruiser: Non-wheeled vehicle used for transportation. Uses an impeller enclosed on the underside for lift, similar to a helicopter.

Cryogenesis: Inducing stasis through the use of extreme cold such as with liquid nitrogen.

Cut Set: Level within a Fault Tree. The first cut set is something that can go wrong and cause a device to fail. The second cut set is something that can cause the first cut set to fail, the third cut set causes the second to fail and so forth, creating a chain reaction of failures.

Cyraria: Fictitious planet orbiting Xi star-system in the constellation Scorpio.

Cyll: Advanced version of an enclosed bed with automatic temperature and support control for comfort like a very advanced Earth mattress.

Cyrarian Space Facility (CSF): Massive spacestation in orbit around Cyrarian where incoming space vehicles dock and passengers obtain transportation to the surface.

D

Dark Matter: Invisible matter in the Universe that has mass and gravity but cannot be seen.

Dark Energy: Energy believed to be present in the Universe which can be converted into matter and thus form stars and planets.

Decarachnid: A ten-legged arachnid or spider.

Devenite: A form of cristobalite which not only facilitates the transmission of psi waves but has the ability to bend time based on input derived from the user's emotional center. Violet in color, the crystal is an intercalation compound which allows it to have chronoviatic (time travel) ability.

Digichronometer: Digital time keeper, i.e. digital clock.

Disinformation: Lies presented as if they are true in order to deceive and mislead others.

Dununda: Underground Cyrarian city in Sigma/Epsilon covered by a massive, transparent dome.

E

Eioatian: Fictitious massive intelligent space slug which can reach tens of meters in length, is devoid of emotion and has a natural distrust of humans.

Electroid: Similar to a robot. Usually shortened simply to 'troid.

Electromagnetic Radiation: The technical term for what we know as light.

Ellipse: An ellipse is similar to a circle except it appears to be stretched out into more of an egg shape. To drawn an ellipse you can place to pins or thumbtacks into a piece of paper on a suitable surface (other than your mother's mahogany dining room table), tie a string to each one and then use the string to guide your path with a pencil. Each of the pins represents a focus (plural = foci). A circle is a special case where the two foci are in the same place or coincident.

Cyraria's orbit around Zeta and Zinni is two ellipses connected in the middle between the two stars so that combined they look like a figure eight, which is also how the planet moves around them. A figure eight shape is known as a lemniscate. Some believe that such an orbit could not exist while others believe it could but it would be very unstable. The determining factor is the gravitational pull of each star. If one is much smaller and therefore likely to be weaker than the other, the other would be able to "steal" the planet and it would orbit one or the other in an elliptical orbit. It would also be possible to orbit them both in a single ellipse with each sun at a focus.

Encephalographic Signature: Fictitious group of brainwave patterns that many people share which tells something about their temperament. Based on the electro-magnetic characteristics of a person's brain. Different than a mindprint which is another level of detail and different for everyone.

Encryption: Scrambling a signal or message into a form that disguises it so that no one else can read or understand it.

Entry Buffers: Spacecraft system that slows and protects the craft from burning up during atmospheric entry or landing on a planet with an atmosphere.

Ephemeris: A listing usually in table form of the positions of planets, moons, stars, the sun at a certain time as well as when events such as eclipses will occur.

Eppy: Slang term used for an Elite Political Prisoner (EPP).

Erebusite: Fictitious race of intelligent humanoids from the star-system Erebus. They possess a strong, stocky build, with scaled, mustard-colored, hairless skin. They have three fingers of equal length and a single eye protected by several, overlapping, horizontal eyelids which adjust like blinds to control light.

Esheron: Fictitious planet continually at war over mineral rights and other planetary assets. The majority of men are fighting the wars while the women run the businesses and much of the governmental functions.

Esheronian Contingency Law: Law on Esheron intended to provide for women whose husbands die in the wars. They can join another family, usually that of a relative, and become an additional wife with permission from the first. Instituted to make sure that war widows are cared for if they are unable to care for themselves.

F

Faster Than Light (FTL): Travel faster than the speed of light, usually achieved by warping space since nothing can travel faster than light which is 186,000 miles per second or 669,600,000 miles per hour.

Fault Tree: Used in engineering to map out everything that can go wrong and cause something to not operate so that something can be done to assure the device will still work.

Federal System: Political organization formed by agreement of its members who can still create most of their own laws while the central power provides such things as a common monetary system, law enforcement and/or various protective services or benefits.

Flashers: Fictitious Cyrarian insects that live in colonies and resemble Earth's cockroaches.

Flauna: Species that combine the characteristics of both plants and animals.

Flora peda telepathis or flora pedis telepathis: A fictitious species of flauna with telepathic abilities. They can also ambulate (walk) on broad-based leaves similar in size and shape to a seal's flippers. Some have judged their intelligence level to exceed that of humans.

Flowstone: Cave or cavern formations forms by water erosion and looking as if they have been melted.

G

Galactic Standard Year (GSY): Fictitious term for creating a standard time measurement. A year is usually defined by the time it takes a planet to make one revolution around its sun but since all planets do so at a different rate, a standard was set at 400 chrons, which is similar to a day but 26 hours long.

Galarium: Similar to a library on Earth but without books, which don't exist anymore. All information is stored on computers in a variety of formats similar to multi-media devices.

Genour: Generic Nourishment. Dry cakes or bars made from stale grain as food when nothing else is available. Similar to Earth's granola bars but not as tasty.

Glyph: A symbol that stands for something specific and is often obvious enough for people to understand, even if they can't read.

Gravitational Assist: Using a planet's gravity to give a spacecraft a boost of energy and thus velocity.

Gravitational Vortex: A place where the gravity from a blackhole, several planets or stars combines in such a way as to create a gravitational whirlpool that could suck in and trap a spacecraft.

Graviton: Tiny theoretical particle presumed to convey the force of gravity.

H

Heat Exchanger: Basic component of an air conditioner which uses a liquid to remove heat from the air. A fluid absorbs the heat until it evaporates, then the steam is taken to another area where it is cooled and condenses back to a liquid, releasing the heat. Then it starts the cycle over again.

Heatlock: An enclosed area at the entrance to a building that keeps extreme heat or cold weather outside from coming in.

Hostii Intergalactic Organization (HIO): Fictitious galactic organization whose primary purpose is to maintain peace between the various star-systems.

Holocube: A data storage device based on holographic layers visible at different angles. Its function is similar to Earth's ebook reading devices.

Holodendril: Fictitious tree on Verdaris with round, crystal-like leaves that reflect light and make a sound like wind chimes.

Holographix: Fictitious patterns and sounds specifically designed to relieve stress and keep a person calm. In private areas they are coded for the individual.

Holoprism: A fictitious device similar in appearance to a crystal which contains thousands of pages controlled by a small wheel on the side.

Holoviewer: Similar to a television except it projects the image into space in 3D.

Hoverisms: Fictitious anti-gravity component used in various ground and space vehicles.

Humanoid: Creature shaped approximately like a human that has two legs, two arms, a single head and walks upright. Intelligence level varies as well as communication ability.

Hyperbolic Orbit: An orbit that isn't closed like those of the Moon, Sun or Earth. Used for a gravitational assist where a spacecraft uses the gravity of a planet or other space object to give it more speed and change direction.

I

Ideology: A belief system usually associated with a specific group.

Inclination: Measurement usually in degrees above the horizon of a star, planet, spacecraft, spacestation, etc.

Infirmary: A place to care for those who are sick or injured but usually lacking less equipment than a hospital.

Interdimensional Excursion: Fictitious term for slipping from one dimension into another, typically through the effects of gravity or relativity.

J

Jendak: A marginally intelligent species shorter than most humans at about a meter and a half tall with purple skin, a rotund body and thin, rodent-like tail. Their face is somewhat flat accented by articulating pointed ears. They do well with simple, repetitive tasks that humans find boring such as assembly work. Many have strong intuitive and psychic abilities as well as excellent mechanical dexterity. Their hands similar to humans with an opposing thumb.

K

Karma: The concept that how you act toward others will eventually come back to you. If you treat others nicely, they will treat you nicely but if you're mean, eventually someone will do the same thing to you.

Keesha: Small animal similar to a rabbit sometimes used for food or fur.

Kepler's Laws of Planetary Motion: Three fundamental physical laws identified by Johann Kepler in the end of the 16th century that describe the motion of any heavenly body orbiting another. The 1st law states that the orbits of planets are elliptical, not circular as originally believed, with the Sun or central body at one of the foci of the ellipse. (See "ellipse.") The second law was that an orbiting body will sweep out equal areas in equal time. What this means is if you were to measure the area between the Earth and the Sun for a specific time period, it will always be the same. The implications of this law are that a planet does not always move at the same velocity but moves faster when closer to the Sun than when it's farther away.

Thus, for Cyraria, it would move through the area between the two stars faster than when it's on the far side of one or the other. The third law states that the period of time a planet takes to orbit the Sun is proportional to the distance from it, linking the two together. The implications of this law are that it doesn't matter what the mass is of an object in orbit. It depends only on the mass of the central body, such as the Sun, and the satellite's distance, meaning that a small satellite or the Moon would move at the same rate if in the same orbit.

Kolkhoz: Self-sustaining communal farm.

L

Lasocular: Fictitious term for laser-directed nuclear energy typically used in weapons.

Lasomag: Fictitious high-powered laser weapon that has an electro-magnetic power source.

The Laws: Common term for the laws on Mira III which directed all aspects of life.

Learning Curve: The time it takes to fully understand a given skill or concept.

Ledorian Order: A religious order based on Esheron that believes in an intelligent creator and the need to maintain positive energy in the Universe to keep it from collapsing.

Lemitini: Herbal substance similar to chocolate with strong healing powers and extremely pleasant flavor.

Lemniscate: A shape like a figure eight. (See "ellipse.")

Local Time: The prevailing time vector on a specific inertial reference frame.

Logarithm: Mathematical term for organizing numbers based on how many times it is multiplied by itself (exponent). For example, logarithms based on 10 would include 10, 100, 1000, etc. while a logarithm based on 2 would be 2, 4, 16, etc.

Luma: Fictitious plant natural to Cyraria which has phosphorescent properties, in other words it glows in the dark and can provide lighting.

Luminal Velocities: The speed of light.

M

Magnavon: Single passenger vehicle similar to a motorcycle but without wheels so it uses magnetic levitation to lift it from the surface.

Magnetic Resonance Device (MRD): Equipment used to scan the interior of an object using the interaction of magnetic fields. Similar to Magnetic Resonance Imagine or MRI used in Earth medical applications.

Magnetometer: Instrument that measures the strength of magnetic fields.

Martial Law: Rule enforced by military action.

Mediveke: Veke used as a combination ambulance and treatment suite. (See veke)

'Merama : Common term for chimera madre which is the Mira III term for mother or mom.

'Merapa: Common term for chimera padre which is the Mira III term for father or dad.

Mindprint: A person's unique signature based on their brain's psi waves which are different from everyone else's and more specific than their encephalographic signature which is based on electromagnetic waves.

Mira III: Fictitious planet in the Mira system which is always foggy, blocking any view of the sun or stars. Its advanced technologies provide various comforts as well as a high level of control by the government which restricts personal freedoms.

MRD: See Magnetic Resonance Device.

Mula: In Vedic tradition a part of the sky known as a lunar mansion which represents a soul's mission to escape the cycle of life and death. It is ruled by the deity, Nittriti, goddess of death and destruction. Mula brings pain which changes a person as they let go of material things and seeks for spiritual knowledge.

Mutogueronian: Sign language developed on Esheron to avoid being heard by audio surveillance devices.

N

Nanobots: Microscopic robots incorporated into everything from fabric to human beings and programmed to perform a specific task, some good to provide comfort and others to induce pain and suffering or some other unpleasant function.

Nanosensors: Microscopic sensors incorporated into fabric and furniture to sense a person's tension level and then provide an appropriate level of comfort.

Naterra: Galactic term for a person's planet of birth.

Navilator: Spacecraft navigation device which contains information about stars, gravity, interstellar storms and so forth.

Negative Energy Spikes: Energy related to or generated by antimatter.

Nifeir: Cyraria's single moon named for its high content of the minerals nickel, iron and iridium.

Noncompliance Report (NCR): Notices issued to students in the Mira III educational system when they break any of the rules, including asking too many questions as well as getting an answer wrong. Offenders were listed on an electronic board to further embarrass those who couldn't follow the rules.

Norfed: Confused.

O

Ocular Refractors: Electronic binoculars.

Oppsuit: Similar to a spacesuit but designed to keep a person at a comfortable temperature during Cyraria's extreme weather, both hot and cold.

Orbital Dynamics: Movement of an object in orbit including its speed and the size of the orbit around a central point such as a planet or star. Also see "Kepler's Laws."

Orbital Mechanics: Mathematical methods used for calculating orbits based on such factors as the mass of both bodies and radial distance. Can be used to predict location at any given time once the cycle parameters are known.

Orthostatic Intolerance: The inability to stand up. Astronauts exercise regularly while in zero gravity for extended missions to prevent this condition. Without the need to bear weight in a gravity field the bones and muscles weaken and atrophe.

P

PEPIR: See Piloting Extrapolation Projection of Input Results.

Perihelion: The bottom of an elliptical orbit or its point closest to the object it's orbiting.

Phase Change: When a substances changes from a solid, liquid or gas to one of the other states or phases. Energy is used or released between stages which can be used in such systems as heat exchangers.

Photoreceptors: Visual sensors on an electroid.

Photosynthesis: The process by which a plant generates energy using light.

Phynques: A carnivorous species of flauna similar to cactus that moves about on hundreds of feet-like roots so it can find food such as insects or other plants.

Physical Assistance and Remediation (PAR): Similar to a doctor's office on Earth but with higher technology, including the ability to treat patients who are not present.

Piloting Extrapolation Projection of Input Results (PEPIR): Computer simulation to determine results of directions given to a spacecraft.

Planetary Law Enforcement Database (PLED): Fictitious computer database where Cyrarian residents' records including school grades or breaking the law are kept.

Pneumatoplasmic: Fictitious term for the properties of dark matter.

22

Portalume: Device similar in function to a flashlight.

Pressure Vortex (PV): Strongly circulating air such as in a tornado. On Cyraria, massive storms which occur when one part of the planet is much colder than another creating convection currents that become twisted by the planet's rotation and result in dangerous tornados much larger than those on Earth.

Promises: Vows taken during Ledorian ceremonies.

Protoplasm: The most basic form of living matter for both plants and animals.

Psaid: Term used when communicating using psi. Similar to the word "said" for when a person talks in the usual way.

Psetora: Fictitious insectoid similar in appearance to a cockroach. They communicate telepathically which allows them to hunt their prey as a group. Their antennae flash orange when all have focused on the same target and are ready to strike.

Psi: The consciousness level of brainwaves which travels faster than light and is how telepathy and other psychic abilities operate.

Psi Link: Telepathic connection between two people communicating using psi waves.

Pubescent Crawler (p-crawler): Creeping plant native to Cyraria that has small, delicate leaves filled with sap which give it insulation properties. However, if broken open, the sap has a very offensive odor.

Pyxisites: Another humanoid species with limited intellect which they compensate for by being sneaky and untrustworthy. Their skin is dark with a greenish cast like tarnished copper, their eyes are deepset, round, amber in color and feline-like with what little hair they have dark and wispy. They hail from the starsystem, Pyxis, which was evacuated as a series of recurrent novas increased in strength until they threatened to annihilate its two habitable planets.

Q

Quadrumvirate: An organization ruled by four rulers or groups.

Quantum Paralysis Device (QPD): A fictitious device similar in function to a refrigerator which inhibits chemical reactions and therefore prevents food spoilage.

Quantum Entanglement: Experiments indicate that when a photon (a particle of light) is split, contact is maintained between the components due to the fact that if the spin of one changes the other portion instantaneously changes as well, indicating some form of communication exists between them. Thus, when a particle such as a photon, electron or even a molecule is "entangled" with another, any influence on one will affect the other instantaneously. This occurs faster than the speed of light which implies its timeless and could possibly be related to or the mechanism of psi phenomena.

R

Radio Frequency (RF): Radio waves or how radios work.

Rakii: Erubesite term for wife.

Refraction: Changing the direction of a wavefront such as light by passing it through a different medium such as a crystal which changes its transmission velocity and direction.

Regional Governor (RG): Top leader for a Cyrarian region which is part of a Territory.

Regionists: Those who live in a specific region.

Regions: Each Cyrarian Territory is divided into 24 regions, each with their own government.

Relativity: Theory developed by Albert Einstein that states that time and space are not constant but can change when something is moving close to the speed of light.

Replicon: A fictitious robot designed to look and act like a specific person, in other words a replica often used as instructors in the Miran Academies.

Rhetoric: How an idea is expressed using a certain style so that it may sound better than it really is.

Rollapeds: Caster-like wheels often used on 'troids and automatons.

S

S3: A network of satellites orbiting Cyraria used to gather information such as weather conditions but also used by some to spy on people's activities.

Sanicube: Bathroom or toilet facilities.

Sapphirans: Sub-human race of humanoids with low intelligence. They believe that plants are better than animals and therefore only eat meat, including people, which makes them cannibals.

Serendipity: Discovering something fortunate unexpectedly; a lucky break.

Shravana: In Vedic tradition a section of the sky known as a lunar mansion. Its message is to listen to the sounds of silence through self-discipline and pursuing the path of truth which allows a person to know whether or not something is real.

Singularra: Miran term for being alone, a concept that does not have cultural approval. Someone who preferred to be alone was considered to be crazy, thus the word was often used in that way as well.

Situational awareness: Paying attention to what is going on around you.

SMC: See Surveillance and Monitoring Capability

Smutch: Fictitious remnant of a blown-out star made of carbon with a diamond core that was eventually captured by another star system and thus considered a planet. In turn it captured one of the system's asteroids which was engineering to be habitable and often used by intragalactic smugglers and other criminals as a rendezvous site.

Snurk: A stupid or foolish person.

Snurkles: Expression of surprise or disbelief.

Spatial Plane: A dimension that is defined by a flat surface such as a table.

Speed of Light: 186,000 miles per second or 1,000,000,000 meters per second. According to Einstein's relativity theory nothing other than light can travel at this speed.

Spickle Tree: Cactus-like plant native to Cyraria that defends itself from predators by hurling spikes when disturbed.

Stalagmite: A column coming up from ground level that results from water dripping through limestone such as in a cavern.

Stalactite: A column coming down from the ceiling from water dripping through limestone such as in a cavern.

Stalii: Grain-like seed that develops in the stalk which ruptures when the seeds are ripe. The stalks are somewhat larger than corn stalks on Earth and the seeds about the size of tennis balls.

Stasis: Suspended animation or chemically induced sleep which slows down bodily processes enough that they can stay alive for long periods of time such as that required for space travel that takes longer than a person's lifetime.

Stungun: Fictitious weapon used to stun people or prey using an electric charge.

Subterre: An underground residence or office where the ground is the primary insulation from heat or cold as well as weather disturbances.

Supply Depot (SD): Government run store where regionists can obtain the supplies they need to build homes or other projects.

Surveillance and Monitoring Capability (SMC): Use of electronic devices to spy on a person as well as measure their reaction by their heartrate, breathing, etc.

Sweeper: Hawk-like Cyrarian bird with a rotating tail that teases its prey prior to eating it in one bite.

Synchronous Orbit: An orbit that is synchronized with the rotational rate of the central body. For example, geosynchronous communication satellites orbiting the Earth take 24 hours to complete one orbit, the same amount of time it takes for the Earth to make a single rotation, thus keeping them in the same location overhead.

T

Tachyonic Transmission: Fictitious means for sending a message faster than the speed of light.

Telepathy: Method for communicating with another person through thought.

Telerobic Surrogates: Robots that duplicate the motion of a human or programmed to perform tasks usually done by humans. Can be used remotely across vast distances for tasks such as surgery.

Terra: Planet located in the Orion Bridge which connects the Perseus and Sagittarius arms of the Hostii (Milky Way) Galaxy. Known commonly as Earth.

Territorial General (TG):   Head of a territory with some level of authority over its 24 regions.

Territories: Geographic divisions on Cyraria that divide it into 6 sectors.

Time Adjustment Station (TAS):   Outposts in space that adjust the time for space travelers which gets distorted due to travel near the speed of light.   The Theory of Relativity explains how when something is moving close to the speed of light that time goes more slowly.   For example, 10 days on a spacecraft could pass while 100 years passes on a planet.   To assure that travelers arrive in the same timeframe, the TAS uses gravity waves to place them in the proper time.

Timebump: Being sent forward or backward in time by a spacecraft malfunction or encounter with a strong gravity field.

Time Dilation: The principle included in Einstein's theory of relativity that time passes slower for objects moving near the speed of light.

Time Dilation Modulator (TDM):   Spacecraft component to adjust for differences in time.   If the TDM's operate properly there is no need for a TAS.

Trajectory: The path of a moving object such as a thrown ball.

Transcription Errors: DNA damage that causes failure of a person's body to come back together properly after being dissolved by a transporter beam or traveling near the speed of light.

Transcrypters: A device used to communicate secretly.   Voices are scrambled or encrypted as one person speaks then translated back for the other person to understand but anyone listening would only hear garbled noise.

Transponder: An electronic device that sends a signal, often from a vehicle, so that others can tell where it is.

Triumvirate: An organization ruled by three separate groups.

'Troid: Common term for an electroid or robot.

Tsesepia: Fictitious planet with a toxic atmosphere used for insecticide.

Turbidity: The amount of particles or sediment in air or water. Relates to the amount of dust in the Cyrarian atmosphere from its dry surface.

Tysa: Fictitious holographic game the object of which is to assemble a variety of different shapes into a single block or shape.

U

Undissipated Charge Differential: Electric charge buildup that can result in an electrical shock.

Universal Time: The prevailing time vector on a specific inertial reference frame.

Uttara Bhadra: In Vedic tradition a section of the sky known as a lunar mansion presided over by Ahir Budhyana, ruler of water and darkness. It represents trouble that is finally solved.

V

Vacushield or Vacshield: Transparent barrier or window in a spacecraft protecting it from the vacuum of space.

Vapora: Fictitious pools of hydrocarbons deposited in the atmosphere by a comet. When they combine with oxygen they become a fire storm.

V-disk: Vector disk used on spacecraft to provide lift and direction.

Vegemal: A creature that combines characteristics of both a plant and an animal. Some have high intelligence, such as Thyron.

Veke: Common term for "vacuum certified vehicle" or VCV. Disk-shaped craft similar to the typical shape of a UFO which can travel on or off a planet, but with limited range. For example, one could be used to travel to a planet's moon but not another planet.

Verdaris: Planet in the Algonian system used primarily for growing food. The system has several comets which hit the planet often making it too dangerous for permanent settlements.

Veridical Dream: A prophetic dream that provides insights and truth that are critical to the receiver's life path.

Videra: An Erubesite's visual sensor or eye that represents their most prominent feature. Multiple, horizontal eyelids adjust according to incoming light intensity, protecting it in harsh environments while still allowing for a moderate amount of night vision.

W

Warp Gully or Warp Run: Naturally occurring route through space that contracts space and expands time due to gravity from various nearby stars or blackholes.

Warp Harmonics: Fictitious spacecraft system designed to fold space gravitationally and virtually shrink distances. Each harmonic level is an order of magnitude or ten times stronger than the one before it.

Wiitiins: Fictitious creatures native to Cyraria which live in hot springs. Similar in size, taste and texture to shrimp.

Wormhole: A tunnel between parts of space that greatly shortens the distance through relativistic effects.

Wrist Wrings: Similar to handcuffs but with the ability to temporarily numb and thus disable the prisoner's hands and arms so they can't use them.

Y

Yraglian Lizard: Colorful hooded fictitious Cyrarian lizard that defends itself by emitting a cloud of gas with an odor that can knock out its prey or enemies.

Z

Zinaanians: This species hails from a starsystem in the constellation known on Earth as Scorpio but is invisible due to the high nebulosity surrounding it. Its natives are highly intelligent with facial features which in some respects resemble a dinosaur. They walk upright on somewhat short but powerful legs, have broad, bull-like shoulders with relatively short but well-muscled arms, hands with three fingers of unequal length and scaled skin which is bronze-colored. Their head is broader at the top with spherical eyes of a reddish hue on either side which rotate independently and thus can attain a three-hundred-sixty degree view while their body remains still. Other facial features include angular, protruding cheeks separated by a thin, bony nose and a relatively wide lipless mouth above a powerful, pointed jaw.

Zodiac: A system of star patterns or constellations which surround a star-system and can be used to mark time based on the view from the planet and where its sun or suns happen to be. Similar to Earth, the Cyrarian zodiac has 12 signs including the Conquerer, Sower, Scholar, Judge, Rock, Destroyer, Healer, Reaper, Accuser,

Psychic/Seer, River and Builder. Each has a meaning related to its name which astrologers interpret and predict future events.

Zones: Scheduling system that determines what time something should occur such as waking up, eating, attending school or work, going to sleep, etc.

Zygodactyl: Having two toes or fingers facing forward and one back such as found in certain birds or Erebusites.

STAR SYSTEM FACTS

Starsystem Class: Binary
Location from Earth: Constellation Scorpio, Xi A & B
Class: F5-IV subgiants

Average Separation: 18 AU (2.6928 x 10^12 meters) (Similar to distance between Uranus and Earth's Sun)
3rd Component: dG7 Orange dwarf, magnitude 7.2, slow retrograde orbit with period of 1000 years

ZETA (Xi A)
Absolute Magnitude: 2.9 (~5x Earth's Sun)
Surface Temperature: 6800K
Mass: 2.88x10^30 kg
Luminosity: 1.95x10^34 erg sec-1
Radius: 1.131x10^6 km

ZINNI (Xi B)
Absolute Magnitude: 3.1
Surface Temperature: 6500K
Mass: 2.66x10^30 kg
Luminosity: 1.87x10^34 erg sec-1
Radius: 1.213x10^6 km

HABITABLE PLANET: Cyraria

Planetary Surface Temperature Range: -53 degrees C/-64 degrees F to 101 degrees C/214 degrees F
Radius: 6.5x10^6 m
Mass: 6.8x10^24 kg
Rotational Period: 26 hours
Axial Inclination: 87 degrees
Gravitational Acceleration: 10.735 meters sec^-2

Distance to Zeta:
2.692×10^8 km aphelion
1.904×10^8 km perihelion
Semi-major axis: 2.02×10^8 km
Eccentricity: .333
Period: 6880 days
Angular Size from Cyraria:
.48 degrees Perihelion
.12 degrees Aphelion

Distance to Zinni:
2.65×10^8 aphelion
1.889×10^8 perihelion
Semi-major axis (Zinni): 1.98×10^8 km
Eccentricity: .326
Period: 7120 days
Angular Size from Cyraria:
.51 degrees Perihelion
.13 degrees Aphelion

Orbital Characteristics
Double ellipse (lemniscate)
Entire Circuit: ~14,000 days

Seasons: 16
Temperature Range: -53C/-64F to 101C/214F
Contiguous Length of Opposition: 778 days (Seasons 12 & 13)
Length of Winter: 3058 days
Galactic Standard Year: 400 days

Planetary Satellites: 1 (Nifeir)

NIFEIR

Orbital Period: 36 days
Radius: 2144.7 km
Average distance from Cyraria: $1.46\text{x}10^5$ km
Composition: Nickel (Ni), Iron (Fe), Iridium (Ir)
Atmosphere: Null

CYRARIAN WEATHER

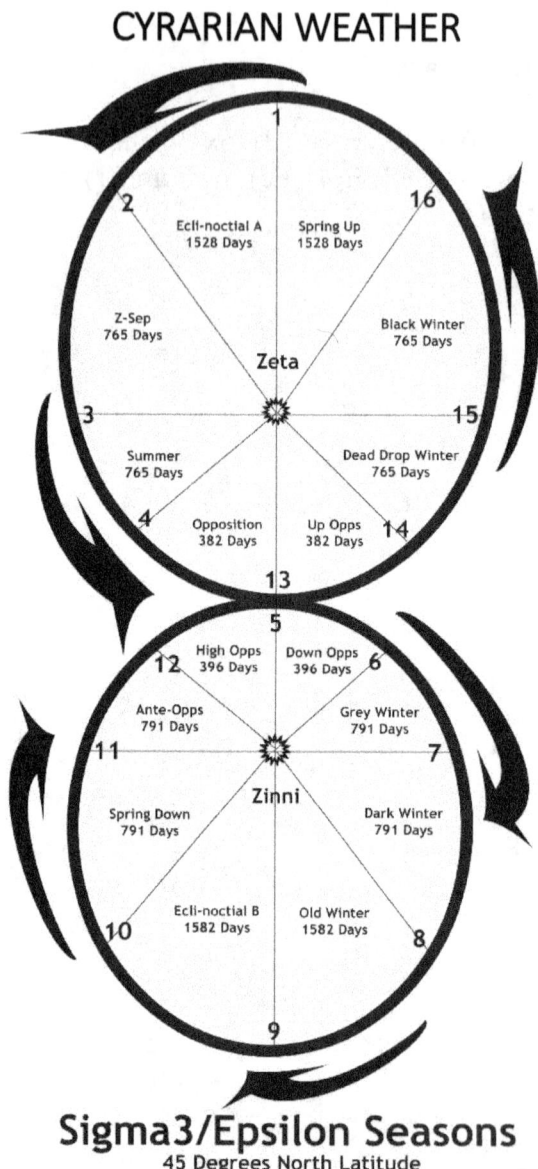

Sigma3/Epsilon Seasons
45 Degrees North Latitude

The climate on Cyraria is one of dramatic extremes, from as cold as -60 degrees Celsius (C)/-76 degrees Fahrenheit (F) to 106 degrees C/222 degrees F. While the lemniscadian orbit is partly to blame, the 87 degrees inclination of the planet's axis is a major factor. Earth is only 23 degrees from the vertical yet this accounts for the seasons as one hemisphere then the other leans toward the Sun. This changes the Sun's declination (height in the sky), making its rays hotter the higher it gets, as well as defining the length of the ecliptic (path across the sky) which determines the number of hours of daylight.

Cyraria, however, is tipped on its side and is thus closer to being horizontal than vertical. Thus there are times when its northern hemisphere is facing either Zeta or Zinni constantly while the southern is in complete darkness and vice versa. Sigma3/Epsilon is at 45 degrees North Latitude so is halfway between the planets north pole and equator. This tempers its seasons slightly versus what it is at extreme locations but still results in dramatic and lethal differences.

The length of the seasons differ dramatically as well. This is due to the nature of elliptical orbits. According to Kepler's 3rd Law of Planetary Motion, a planet will sweep out "equal area in equal time." The illustration at the top of this section is not to scale but you can get the idea that when the planet is between Zeta and Zinni in its Opposition period the area shown is relatively small compared to that at the opposite ends, such as its Ecli-noctial periods.

Thus, the planet actually moves faster in its orbit during the smaller sectors than the larger ones. This is fortunate considering that Opposition temperatures are extremely high. Furthermore, when the planet is between the two stars it undergoes tremendous gravitational forces in opposite directions which could tear it apart. At the least it will experience groundquakes and various other disturbances during this relatively short but precarious time which has a duration of over two Earth years.

A lemniscadian orbit is unstable and highly unlikely to occur. The theory behind it is that the third component of the star system, a dG7 orange dwarf star with an orbital period of a thousand years, nudged it into that configuration. It's possible the next pass could pull it back to a simple ellipse around both stars, depending on the planet's location at the next transit.

Temperature extremes between the north and south hemispheres contribute to severe weather such as pressure vortices (PVs), or tornados as they're known on Earth. When cold air and hot air mix the convection forces can form a funnel as the hot air rises and cold air drops. The temperatures would be even more extreme if it weren't for the thick atmosphere which contains a significant amount of dust. During the PV season more dust is stirred up which actually helps opposition temperatures from being even higher.

SEASONS

1. Equi-noctial A: GROWING SEASON. Temperature Range: 17 – 31C/63-88F (1528 Days) Zeta and Zinni are in conjunction. Zeta predominates by distance and thus completely occludes Zinni. It is cooler in Sigma/Epsilon because of its latitude with Zeta rising and setting with light and darkness equal but Zeta skims the horizon as the season begins. As it progresses, Zeta rises higher, increasing the heat. Halfway into this season Zeta has risen halfway up the sky but day and night remain equal. While this season is long enough for numerous crops to be grown at these temperatures, until irrigation systems are developed there are still numerous challenges.

2. Z-Separation: WAXING HEAT SEASON. Temperature Range: 27 – 47C/ 81-117F (765 Days) During this season Zeta and Zinni begin to separate in the sky, i.e. Zinni gradually becomes visible, which explains the season's name. However, it is small at this stage because it is very far away, i.e. approximately six times as far as the orbit of Pluto. It will appear as a bright star or similar to Venus at maximum elongation. By the end of this season Zeta will be high in the sky but not directly overhead at Sigma's latitude, providing strong light and heat, warming things up quickly. The days continue to lengthen until Zeta is in the sky constantly, sweeping a huge circle in the sky. From this point there will be constant daylight for the equivalent of several Earth years.

3. Summer: HOT. Temperature 47 – 65C/ 117-149F (765 Days) Zeta remains in a circumpolar orbit such that it never sets which means the surface never cools. Furthermore, Cyraria is approaching it's closest proximity to Zeta which drives the heat up even more. Zinni visibly rises and sets as it grows larger and more noticeable as opposed to an extremely bright star.

4. Opposition: WAY TOO HOT. Temperature 65 - 80C/ 149 - 176F (382 Days) Zeta's path across the sky is a tilted ellipse which will eventually set for brief periods but by this time Zinni is about the same distance away and rises at the time. Certain parts of the day both are in the sky, driving surface heat into and even more lethal range. Groundquake season begins due to the pull of opposing gravity from Zeta and Zinni.

5. Down* Opposition: EXTREME DROP FROM HOT TO COLD. Temperature 2 - 80C/ 36 - 176F (396 Days) As this season begins Cyraria is directly between Zeta and Zinni where the lemniscate crosses. Both rise and set, one after the other, so that one is always in the sky. Sigma/Epsilon is spared the worst of this period due to its high latitude so that neither sun is directly overhead. Both are at approximately 45 degrees.

The continual light, however, doesn't allow the surface to cool so it remains hot during this time. However, the transition to cooler weather comes quickly as the planet progresses into the portion of its orbit around Zinni. This sudden drop begins another Pressure Vortex or PV season due to temperature extremes. Groundquakes are less frequent. Zeta and Zinni continue to drop in the sky, one rising as the other sets, until each only scrapes the horizon, their light casting long shadows. (*Down refers to start of Zinni orbit.)

6. Grey Winter: TOO COLD. Temperature 2C to -42C/36 to -43F (791 Days) Zeta has shrunk to the size of brilliant star its heat negligible and Zinni is now entirely below the horizon.

7. Dark Winter: EXTREME COLD Temperature -42C to -50C/ -43F to -58F (791 Days) Zeta reaches 10 degrees above the southwest horizon so Sigma/Epsilon is in low light when it is above the horizon. Zinni is below the horizon. Temperature differential between the North and South hemispheres is substantial and results in PV's along equatorial regions. This violent mix of hot and cold air as well as the atmosphere keep it from getting even colder.

8. Old Winter: COLD. Temperature 15C to -50C/59F to -58F (1582 Days) Zeta is to far away to give much light or heat. It is still cold, but begins to warm up again. Zinni gradually begins to rise again, skirting the horizon at first and gradually reaching high in the sky. Temperature variations between the North and South hemispheres continue to generate PV's along the equatorial band but they are less severe as the planet gradually moves toward equal temperatures in both hemispheres.

9. Equinoctial B: GROWING SEASON. Temperature 15 – 30C/ 59-86F (1582 Days) Equal day and night returns. Zinni is visible but eclipsing Zeta for the first part of the season, then gradually separates with both rising and setting at approximately the same time.

10. Spring Down: HOT. Temperature 30C - 38C/86F - 100F (791 Days) Zinni is overhead and never sets in a lopsided circumpolar orbit that ranges from the horizon to zenith. Zeta is visible as it rises then sets but still far away. It is gradually warming up but once again PVs due to the temperature difference between the hemispheres are adding dust to the atmosphere, deflecting some of the heat.

11. Ante Opps: HOTTER. Temperature 38C - 50C/100F - 122F (791 Days) Zinni is in a 45 degree circumpolar orbit. Zeta rises in the northwest, its heat apparent as it adds to Zinni, and is high in the sky at "noon." The weather is warming up very fast.

12. High Opps: WAY TOO HOT. Temperature 50C - 106C/122F - 222F (396 Days) As High Opps begins, Zinni is circumpolar from the horizon to the zenith. Zeta rises in the northwest and reaches a high declination. At times both are visible in the sky in opposite directions. Temperatures rise rapidly in the Northern hemisphere and they continue to cool in the Southern, generating violent PVs. Groundquakes resume. This is the hottest season of the circuit for Sigma/Epsilon. [NOTE:--This is when the Brightstars arrived.]

13. Up* Opps: TOO HOT TO COLD. Temperature 7C - 101C/45F - 214F (382 Days) Zinni and Zeta chase each other across the sky, one or the other visible at all times. They begin this season directly overhead, but their declination gradually drops, each barely peeking over opposite horizons. This is a similar position to Down Opps (5). (*Up refers to leaving the space between Zeta and Zinni to head into orbit around Zeta.) [NOTE:--This is the season when Creena arrived.]

14. Dead Drop Winter: TOO COLD. Temperature 7C to -46C/45 to -51F (765 Days) Neither Zinni nor Zeta rise but Zinni provides a hint of dusk a few hours each day. Once both drop below the horizon it cools quickly. The transition from Up Opps offers a short growing season with mild temperatures.

15. Black Winter: WAY TOO COLD. Temperature -46C to -60C/-51F to -76F (765 Days) Zeta is still invisible while Zinni rises a few degrees above the horizon but is too far away to provide much light and heat.

16. Spring Up: PREPARE FOR GROWING SEASON. Temperature -60C to 17C/-76F to 63F (1528 Days) As the season begins, Zeta is just below the horizon which provides a constant state of dusk. Zinni is rising and setting halfway up the sky but is too far away to provide much warmth. As this season ends, Zeta and Zinni are conjoined again with equal day and night. Zeta is strong enough to warm the planet sufficiently for another growing season.

Note that 15 Earth years elapse between the end of one growing season and the start of the next. However, other areas of the planet experience entirely different seasons and can fill the gaps with imports, allowing Cyraria to be self-sufficient, provided the territories cooperate with one another through trade agreements. Territories which are under Integrator control could be directed not to export to territories that aren't, making food production and its distribution a political tool.

CALMANAC

The Calmanac, as the name implies, is a combination between a calendar and an almanac which contains information relative to the season, how many days have elapsed and how many remain. Weather predictions are included as well which include temperature, dust levels, ultraviolet levels and the risk of a pressure vortex or ground quake occurring. As with all planets, conditions vary depending on latitude, i.e., the distance above or below the planet's center point or equator.

Since the length of the seasons is long, many are divided into sub-seasons the provide further information, such as Peak Opps, which is the most severe portion of the heat season.

The Ephemeris section provides information relative to the position of the two suns, Zeta and Zinni, such as whether it is in a cycle where it will rise and set, remain above the horizon the entire day (circumpolar) or never rise and remain below the horizon (sub-horizonal).

CYRARIAN CALMANAC
45° North Latitude

CURRENT	Sub-season	Sequential	Remaining
Anteopps 779		779/791	12
NEXT	**Sub-season**	**Sequential**	**Remaining**
High Opps		0/396	-12
	Peak (HO132-264)	0/132	-144
CONDITIONS	**Max**	**Min**	**Probability**
Temperature	39°C/103°F	38°C/101°F	99%
Dust	Med-High	Med	87%
UV	High	High	100%
Pressure Vortices (PVs)			34%
Quakes			45%

EPHEMERIS

ZETA ξα	⊛	ZINNI ξβ	⊛

LEGEND	
Rise/Set	☉
Circumpolar (CP)	⊛
Sub-Horizonal	⬤

POLITICAL STRUCTURE

Cyrarian Territories
Epsilon Regional Map

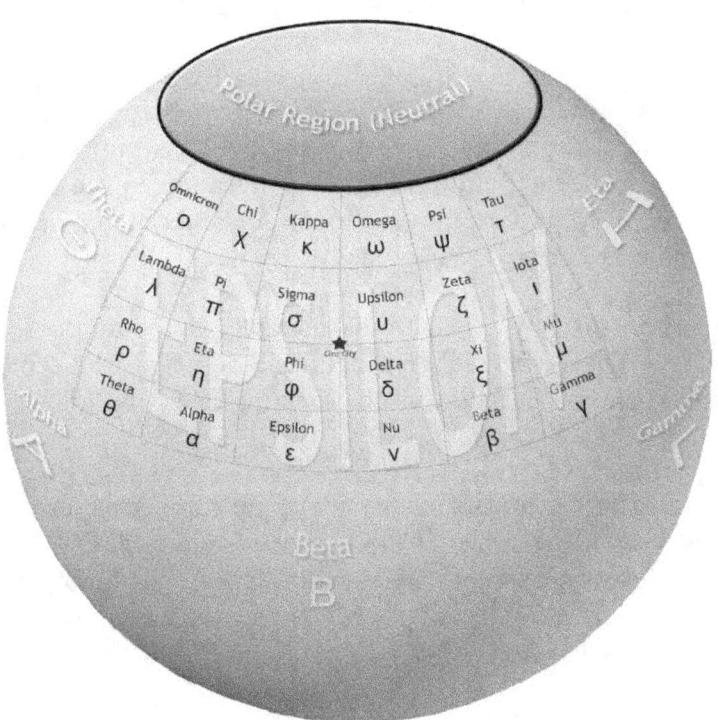

TERRITORIES

Newly settled planets within the Hostii Galaxy are first facilitated by the Hostii Interplanetary Organization, commonly known as the HIO. Typically the planet is divided into 6 territories of equal size with three in each hemisphere. The Territorial Government must answer to the HIO and be in harmony with their charter in order to receive assistance, mostly in the form of imports such as food and other commodities.

Initially the government is primarily a facilitator charged to encourage and mediate communication between regions with regard to commerce and trade. Border disputes are also arbitrated at the territorial level. The territories capital is located in the center in what is considered a neutral region. The polar regions are also neutral as are any moons.

The territory provides various services each region may utilize while financing it accordingly. These include institutions such as hospitals, prisons, law enforcement, immigration, space facilities in the form of space stations to serve incoming and outgoing spacecraft and a shuttle system to the capital.

The territory is led by a Territorial General elected by the Regional Governors. The Territorial General has a deputy who becomes the Territorial General in the event the existing one is no longer able to serve.

If two-thirds of the territories (4) adopt the same structure then the entire planet will be subject to that type of rule with the leadership from each territory having equal say and power via an organization known as a Quadrumvirate. If only three territories combine they are known as a Triumvirate but do not have global power.

REGIONS

Each territory is divided into twenty-four regions of equal size, each initially twenty degrees latitude and twenty degrees longitude though these boundaries may be adjusted as settlement proceeds. They are given names in the order in which they are settled.

The true government under which Cyrarian residents live is determined at the regional level. The HIO allows for the citizens of each region to determine for themselves by popular vote which type of government the wish to be ruled.

If two-thirds of the regions (16) all decide upon the same type of government, then the entire territory can be declared subject to that particular government.

Regional Governors are elected by popular vote and like Territorial Generals have a deputy who will also replace them if unable to complete their term. They assemble their own staff comprising various ministers in accordance with the type of governmental structure decided upon by popular vote of their citizens.

INDIGENOUS POPULATION

THE BNOLAR

At one time Cyraria had surface water which evaporated when the orbit changed from a stable ellipse around Xi's two major components to the current lemniscate, an unstable figure-8 pattern. The change was triggered by the star system's third component, a dG7 orange dwarf which orbits the other two in a period of approximately 1000 years. The additional gravitational effects of its most recent pass were enough to nudge the planet into the current configuration a few hundred years before the arrival of humans.

During the first transit between the two suns, Zeta and Zinni, the surface water was lost but fortunately the underground system of aquifers survived, some replenishing a few surface lakes and rivers during certain seasons in middle latitude regions. The near-collision was also responsible for changing Cyraria's axial orientation from one that was nearly vertical to its current one which is only 13 degrees from the orbital plane, which is the largest factor in the extreme differences in weather during its circuit around the two stars.

The bnolar are the only intelligent creatures native to Cyraria which have been there for millions of years. Their exact population is unknown but estimated to be in the billions. They have survived planetary disasters, weather and tectonic disturbances as well as environmental challenges by living underground in the planet's rich network of caverns.

A unique race not found elsewhere in the galaxy, they stand as tall as approximately two and a half meters though the average is closer to slightly over two meters. They have two massive hind legs and six arms with scoop-like hands ideal for expanding or extending existing tunnels. Their multilayered skin surrounds them like a cloak and serves to reflect different wavelengths of light, protecting them from the harsh environment. Several layers of eyelids do the same for their eyes, which are capable of navigating using infrared wavelengths underground, precluding the need for a subterranean light source other than that provided by luma, a native plant with phosphorescent qualities.

Their society is homogenous and entirely without social strata, largely due to their telepathic and empathic abilities. Each individual bnolar operates within their collective consciousness, making them peaceful and non-aggressive. It is believed that these capabilities originally evolved from their constant exposure to cristobalite which expanded their original communication abilities to include telepathic, empathic and telekinetic skills. These abilities ultimately became reciprocal with the crystals, creating a strong bond between the race's presence and psi conductive properties of local cristobalite sources.

The Think Tank is one of many similar chambers where the energy reflects synergistically within the chamber itself then further energized by the local populace. Being peaceful, the bnolar avoid contact with humans, for whom they wisely hold a high degree of distrust. However, being telepathic as well as empathic they can read a person's mind, emotions and heart and thus determine intent, allowing them to selectively interact with individuals with whom they feel compassion and trust. Their typical family unit is monogamous with pairs mating for life, which is usually over two hundred galactic standard years. Mated pairs tend to have a single child approximately every ten years.

The caverns in which they live form a network beneath 89% of the planet's surface area. Colonies range in size from a few dozen to several hundred thousand, depending on location and available resources. Food supplies comprise that obtained by foraging native plants and herbs when seasonally available some of which are stored for use during extreme weather. Underground sources fill the gap during severe seasons and include fungal species similar to mushrooms, roots, and other vegetation with low light requirements, i.e. those that don't require photosynthesis. If food shortages occur, hibernation is also an option.

STAR TRAILS TETRALOGY BOOK DESCRIPTIONS

BEYOND THE HIDDEN SKY (Volume I)

Moving to another planet is never easy. It's even harder when you never arrive...

Laren Brightstar knew refusing to work for Augustus Troy would make him a target. Being reassigned to the chief terralogist position for Cyraria, a planet on the other side of the galaxy, seemed the perfect solution. Getting there, however, isn't. Not with a teenage daughter like Creena.

She's intelligent.

She's a rebel.

And now she's missing.

In deep space.

Was it an accident? Or abduction?

Either way, he has to find her. Before Troy does. And somehow he knows life will never be simple again as increasingly suspicious circumstances scatter his family across the galaxy, each wondering if they'll survive long enough to be reunited ever again.

A DARK OF ENDLESS DAYS (Volume II)

Things are never so bad they can't get worse. For the Brightstars, they just did...

Cyraria's lethal weather extremes challenge Laren's engineering skills to the max, but his family will perish unless he can build a heat exchanger (air conditioner) to keep their meager ballome at livable temperatures during Opposition. Before its completion, however, old debts come due, leaving his son, Dirck, to complete the task. But how can he possibly do so with no money and limited engineering know-how?

Meanwhile, Creena's situation isn't much better. Her attempt to return to Mira III for help as directed by her father is foiled when the planet on which they expect to find starship passage not only can't help but confiscates their ship. Will she remain trapped forever on a backward and alien world called Earth where she's being pursued by mysterious and hostile forces?

A PSILENT PLACE BELOW (Volume III)

What if you had to kill someone you love before you could save him?

Taking refuge in Cyraria's network of caverns to survive Opposition, Dirck and his mother share a cryptic dream that promises death or worse for his imprisoned father unless immediate action is taken. Will the daring and potentially lethal rescue Dirck and his friend, Win, fabricate succeed or will Laren be lost forever?

The planet's political turmoil increases as the Integrator pursues planetary domination through devious and aggressive means. The formation of an opposition group to fight these hostile actions delivers heavy consequences while additional threats to the Brightstar family at a more personal level arise in the form of cultural clashes between Mira III and Esheron. Creena's return partially reunites the family at last, but ongoing disagreements with her brother distract them from issues that have even more dire consequences.

REFRACTIONS OF FROZEN TIME (Volume IV)

When time is against you, you have one option...

Creena and her little brother, Deven, believe the cavern's crystals can reunite their family at last, including bringing back their father who's on a prison ship heading for permanent exile. Before she can unlock their secrets, however, Integrator forces find their underground hideout, forcing a harrowing escape loaded with unexpected consequences. The lonely days that follow change Dirck forever while also revealing what drives the crystals' ability to manipulate time.

Meanwhile, Laren has discovered the ship's dirty little secret which he hopes to exploit while back on Cyraria, his long-time nemesis, Augustus Troy, not only gains more power than ever before but acquires a weapon capable of wiping out anyone opposed to his despotic goals.

Do the Brightstars have what it takes to survive their final confrontation with the Integrator and his evil proponents? Or will the family's longed-for reunion take place in another dimension of time and space? Find out in this suspense-laden conclusion to the Star Trails Tetralogy.

ABOUT THE AUTHOR

MARCHA FOX IS A SCIENCE FICTION fan and writer who has always been fascinated by space and time. She's an oldtime *Star Wars* nut whose favorite movies include *Back to the Future* and *Deja-vu*. Her life-long love of astronomy eventually drove her to obtain a Bachelor of Science Degree in physics from Utah State University followed by a career of over 21 years at NASA's Johnson Space Center in Houston, Texas, where she held a variety of positions including technical writer, engineer and eventually manager. Needless to say during that time she got to see all sorts of very cool NASA stuff in locations that included Florida, California, Alabama, and Maryland as well as the European Space Agency in The Netherlands.

Her physics training allowed her to "do the math" regarding various elements in her books, especially Cyraria's starsystem, orbital dynamics and resulting seasons in *A Dark of Endless Days*, to assure reasonable accuracy along with hoping to instill an interest in science and engineering to her fans by showing its relevance in an entertaining way. More detailed information as well as a discussion guide for parents and educators are included on her website at **http://www.StarTrailsSaga.com**.

She's the mother of six grown children, seventeen grandchildren and so far three great-grandchildren though she denies being old enough to have such a huge progeny.

CONNECT WITH MARCHA VIA SOCIAL MEDIA:

Author Facebook: https://www.facebook.com/marchafoxauthor
Author Homepage: http://www.StarTrailsSaga.com
Twitter: https://twitter.com/startrailsIV
Blog Page: http://marcha2014.wordpress.com/
Bublish Author Page: https://www.bublish.com/author/view/3111
Tumblr: http://startrailsiv.tumblr.com
LinkedIn: www.linkedin.com/pub/marcha-fox/86/440/326/
Google+:http://www.google.com/+MarchaFoxAuthor
Pinterest: http://www.pinterest.com/kallioperisingp/
YouTube:
https://www.youtube.com/channel/UCZsgOqTmtMFutwU3lt4RByQ

DISCUSSION & LESSON PLAN SUGGESTIONS

Star Trails contains various lessons which are likely to be missed by casual readers. If used as part of a learning module those lessons can be pointed out and used as discussion points. Everyone makes mistakes, even adults, and it is much more effective to learn vicariously from those made by others, particularly fictitious characters, than make the same mistake yourself. This is also an opportunity to explore the science aspects in greater detail as part of science class curriculum or even explore the world of metaphysics. What follows is a summary of lessons contained in various chapters with suggested discussion topics that can prompt assignment ideas.

VOLUME I: BEYOND THE HIDDEN SKY

- Family dynamics: How sibling quarrels can produce dire consequences, i.e. be careful what you wish for.

- Right-brain or left-brain, logic versus intuition and its affect on learning style and communications.

- Consequences of impulsive behavior.

- Assumptions can bring considerable risks when not backed by facts.

- Being responsible for one's choices as well as their affect on others.

- Basics of Kepler's Laws of orbital dynamics and Newton's Laws of motion.

- Einstein's Special and General Relativity theories and their application to space travel including time dilation and theory behind warp drive technology.

- Effects of zero gravity, need for countermeasures to maintain physical strength.

Chapters 1 - 2

1. Creena and Dirck clearly don't get along. What are their basic differences?

Creena is driven by feelings, emotion and intuition while Dirck prides himself on being logical. Is one approach better? Why?

2. Creena is upset and frustrated by the conditions onboard the Aquarius. There is no privacy which is part of the problem but in addition the technology on Mira III helped mitigate feelings through "holographix" which offered soothing colors and sounds as well as other environmental effects to keep people calm. Do you think that such technologies would help control emotions? What is the difference between controlling and suppressing?

3. Creena wants to get away from everyone. Some individuals need solitude to "recharge" and others seek out friends or activities. Which one are you?

4. What was the first mistake that Creena made? Did she know it was wrong? How did she rationalize her decision? When you have to talk yourself into doing something is it usually right or wrong? How much was driven by logic and how much by emotion?

5. Once inside the escape pod did she immediately know what it was? Why not?

It looked like a mini-learning module

6. What additional mistakes did she make? What had her father told her that would have kept her from activating the pod if she had followed his advice?

7. The INTEGRATOR notes that "Mirans were so very easy to deceive." Why?

They are predictable in their actions.

Chapter 3

1. Why didn't a word for "panic" exist on Mira III? Would it be possible to create such a world? Why or why not?

Everything was predictable and controlled so everyone always knew what to expect.

2. What was one thing Dirck liked about Mira III?

All choices were made for him; everything was predictable; they had luxurious living conditions.

3. Dirck's view of life was binary in nature, i.e. "black and white." When does this strategy work and when does it fail to yield accurate information? Why?

Not everything in life is clear. For example, different cultures can believe in traditions that are unacceptable to another. It works for situations where there is a definitive answer only, such as a simple arithmetic problem.

4. Why does Dirck have trouble speculating where Creena might be?

In a black and white world there are fewer options. He's not used to thinking in terms of numerous choices and outcomes.

5. Dirck starts to feel guilty for provoking Creena. Why? Whose fault is it, his or hers?

Everyone is ultimately responsible for their own actions. In spite of the fact he provoked her, she made the choices that resulted in her situation.

6. What does his father mean when he says "To start your off-world education?"

Situations beyond what he experienced on Mira III will be entirely different.

7. Creena experiences stronger emotions than she's ever had when she realizes what has happened. What was the cause?

Adrenaline triggering a "fight or flight" reaction.

Can such a reaction be controlled? Why or why not?

8. It doesn't feel as if the pod is moving. Why?

When something is moving in a straight line at constant speed you can't tell it's moving. This relates to Newton's 1st Law of motion or the principle of inertia which states that an object will remain in a state of rest or constant velocity unless acted upon by unbalanced forces. Newton's 2nd Law is best described by the equation Force = mass x acceleration or $F = ma$.

In other words, the force exerted on an object depends on its mass and how fast it is changing speed or accelerating. Newton's 3rd Law relates to opposing forces, that whenever a force is applied to something, an equal and opposite force is generated, such as the kickback on a rifle or pushing off the side of a swimming pool.

9. Why is Creena weightless in the pod?

It doesn't have a "gravity simulator." Mass such as that of a planet creates gravity which is proportional to how big it is. Scientists still don't understand exactly how or why gravity works but they can predict its strength based on the mass of an object or planet.

10. Mira III had a very ordered way of life which included specific "zones" for each activity. Everything was organized and happened

according to plan. What would it be like to live on such a planet? Would you like it or not? Why?

Chapters 4 - 5

1. Why is Dirck upset by his father's reaction to Captain Troy?

2. Who is on the offensive and who is on the defensive in this encounter?

Both Troy and Laren are on the offensive but Troy's case is stronger. He's in a position of authority and using it to full advantage.

3. Why is Laren so frustrated? Is there more to it than Creena's disappearance?

He had promised his bondling (wife) they would stay on Mira III where she had always lived and everything was predictable. He knew she would be very upset and blame him because they'd had to leave, thus violating his Promises.

4. Why would they need "inertial time adjustments?"

According to Einstein's Theory of Special Relativity time moves at a different rate for objects moving extremely fast, such as near the speed of light which is 186,000 miles per second. In theory, nothing can move faster than the speed of light but time will "dilate" or stretch and expand when something is moving close to that speed. In other words, time progresses at a different rate in a spacecraft traveling near the speed of light. "Inertial time adjustments" would assure arriving in the same dimension of time from which they left as opposed to one in the far future or past.

The fictitious "warp harmonics" referred to in the story relate to Einstein's Theory of General Relativity which states that space can be folded, thus shortening the distance which decreases the time required to reach a given destination.

The physics equation for how far you will go at a certain speed in a certain amount of time is velocity multiplied by time = distance [vt=d] or velocity = distance divided by time [v=d/t]. Distance divided by time is expressed in the common expression "miles per hour." A "base-ten logarithmic scale" refers to a system where each step adds an order of magnitude by multiplying a number by 10, 100, 1000, 10,000, etc.

5. What is one of the primary motivations Laren has to rescue Creena other than the fact she's his daughter?

He made vows "to protect and shield from harm of any kind."

6. Why is Dirck so confused by what happened in Troy's office?

Unquestioned compliance or obedience was of primary importance on Mira III. There were no other options. Now they have a dilemma because the "authority figure" (Troy) has denied any help in finding his sister which violates his father's ability to fulfill his Promises.

7. What does Laren mean that "higher laws" govern his Promises?

Basic human rights to freedom and safety are in the category of "inalienable rights" and thus at a different level that civil or governmental law which should first and foremost protect those it serves, not jeopardize them.

8. When faced with a problem why is it important to identify a "primary objective?"

It helps measure all actions in terms of achieving a specific goal and prevents diversions.

Chapter 6

1. Can you see the stars where you live? If so, how do they make you feel? What would it be like to live on a planet where you never see the sky?

2. Why would it be difficult to have a luxurious life and then suddenly lose it?

3. How does Laren turn the tables on Troy?

Troy's original premise was that the starship was a military craft under military rule. Laren points out that when it's being used as a civilian craft it falls under different laws and regulations related to passenger safety. Since safety requirements were violated, at least part of Creena's disappearance is Troy's fault. This relates also to the responsibility of manufacturers to provide a safe product and assume liability if someone is hurt by it.

4. Why does Troy initially refuse and then agree to provide Laren with a ship to look for Creena?

He has an ulterior motive.

5. On one hand Laren is trying to teach Dirck to think and make choices, then tells him he needs to follow orders. Why this discrepancy?

There are some conditions where someone needs to be in charge for the good of all concerned, particularly when a wrong action by one person could harm the others.

6. Why is Sharra so confident they'll find Creena and bring her home?

Her Miran upbringing has conditioned her to expect a positive outcome with no other options.

Chapters 7- 8

1. Creena's determination to find food and other facilities onboard the pod drive her to do things that a "typical Miran" probably would not. Why?

Mirans always wait to be told what to do. Initiative and original thought were discouraged. What are the pros and cons of such a culture?

2. Why is life in a weightless state different than on Earth?

Gravity forces your body to continually compensate for it by building additional strength. Without it muscles weaken, including the heart, also a muscle, which needs to pump blood against it. "Orthostatic intolerance" is the technical term for not being able to stand up without holding onto something. Astronauts in space exercise to maintain their strength so that when they return to Earth they are not too weak to walk. Some astronauts who have returned from long-duration space flight have not been able to walk without assistance.

Gravity is something we take for granted. For example, pouring a glass of water requires gravity to deliver the liquid to the container. In space the liquid would spill out into the air and float around in a glob. Think about things you do that you can't do upside down and you will discover various "gravity assisted functions." Astronauts often suffer from space sickness, similar to motion sickness, because gravity is not helping keep food and liquids in their stomach.

3. The brain is divided into two parts called "hemispheres," one right, one left. The right side is associated with creativity while the left side is associated with logic and linear thinking. Most people are prone to use one side more than the other. Some believe that people who are left-handed are right-brained while those who are right-handed are left-brained since each side of the brain relates to the opposite side of the body. However, this is not always the case even though those who are left-handed seem more likely to be right-brained.

4. Why would engineers design important systems so that they are "two-fault tolerant?"

So if two fail the other one will still work and not cause a problem.

5. Was Laren's intent in taking Dirck along really a punishment?

Not entirely. However, it would show him the consequences of Creena's loss, in which he played a part. It would also expose him to a situation where decisions and choices were required, with which Dirck had little or no experience.

6. Was Creena doing anything wrong when she tried to figure out where the pod was going? Why did she think it might be? Why was her behavior being observed?

On Mira III initiative and unique questions were punished because they disrupted the status quo. Her behavior was being observed to determine how intelligent and creative she was in addressing problems in spite of growing up on Mira III.

7. Why is it difficult for Dirck to consider what might happen when the arrive on Verdaris?

Everything was predictable on Mira III. If you always knew what was going to happen because it was planned out for you by someone else, how would that affect your ability to make decisions? How would you like to live on a world like that?

Chapters 9 - 11

1. Is there a reason the pod's systems are not working properly?

Yes. The people observing Creena's behavior want to see how she'll react to surprises, whether she'll try to fix them, be as compliant as possible without them, or simply do what she wants.

2. What are the different types of learning styles?

Visual, auditory, and kinesthetic. A visual learner absorbs the most from what they see; an auditory learner does best from listening to others; a kinesthetic learner does best by doing and participating in an activity. It's important to know your primary learning style even though you may not always have a choice on how information is presented. You can still seek out supplemental information in your preferred format to reinforce the data through more efficient means.

3. Why did the inside of the pod get hot when it entered the Verdarian atmosphere?

The air created drag and friction against the surface generated heat. The faster an object is going the more air particles it encounters in less time, increasing the effects. Something going slowly, such as a car, doesn't notice it as much, but this is why windshields are slanted into what is known as an "aerodynamic" shape so there is less air resistance which constitutes a force holding the car back, even if it's small. Race cars are always designed for as little wind resistance as possible, including having a clean, shiny surface.

The insulation and reflective properties of the pod were not sufficient to compensate so the inside heated up. Spacecraft that re-enter an atmosphere require insulation or some other method to keep them from burning up. This is partly why the Space Shuttle, Columbia, was destroyed on February 1, 2003. When it launched a piece of foam from the external tank broke off and cracked the protective material on the leading edge of the wing. When Columbia entered Earth's atmosphere the hot gases entered the inside of the wing, melted the metal frame and caused it to fall off with the entire vehicle subsequently breaking up.

Chapters 12 - 14

1. Are "timebumps" possible?

Theoretically, yes. When technologies are developed that allow for travel at relativistic speeds if malfunctions occur it's possible that time could be disturbed. A "Time Adjustment Station" or TAS could likewise use these technologies to send a vehicle or object to a specific point in time.

2. Why would anyone want to control time?

If you could go backward and forward in time you could determine what was going to happen in the future and then go back and work it to your advantage, such as finding out what number would be drawn in a lotto and then choose that number. However, there are various paradoxes associated with time travel. The most common one is going back in time and killing your grandfather which would mean you would never be born.

Some physics theories such as the "many worlds" or "multiverse" theory state that doing so creates another possibility and therefore another dimension where the new chain of events play out. Some believe that every possible choice anyone can make is active in another dimension.

3. Why would Verdaris have a purple sky?

It's composed of a different combination of gases than Earth, where the predominance of nitrogen causes it to appear blue. A planet's atmosphere reflects light, the color dependent on its wavelength, which in turn relates to the specific type of gas molecule reflecting the light. If a space object doesn't have an atmosphere then the sky would be black, like it is at night, even if it were close to a star like our Sun.

Chapters 15 - 17

1. What is a "tachyonic transmission?"

Some physicists believe that the speed of light is a barrier of sorts for physical material but it's possible that something can actually move faster than light. This is the world of tachyons. If they exist, future technologies could determine how to use it to transmit data in what could be an instantaneous manner. Most data on Earth, particularly what you see, is conveyed through tiny light particles known as photons, which move at the speed of light. For example, the light from the Sun, which is 93 million miles away, takes approximately 8 minutes to arrive on Earth. In other words, if the Sun were to suddenly die, it would be 8 minutes before those of us on Earth would know.)

2. What is wrong with Verdaris?

The fictitious planet is being bombarded by huge pieces of a comet. When huge pieces of space rock or ice enter the atmosphere they heat up from friction like the pod and often explode from rapid expansion, causing significant damage on the planet's surface. It was such a collision which is believed to have wiped out the dinosaurs 63 million years ago.

3. Is there such a thing as warp gullies?

They are possible based on Einstein's Theory of General Relativity. Such a gravitational effect that warps time and space could be caused by a very massive but small object such as a black hole or neutron star. All physical matter is made of atoms which are so small they cannot be seen with the naked eye.

However, there is a lot of empty space within an atom. If a hydrogen atom were made big enough that the nucleus was the size of a softball, its single electron would be 6 miles away. Thus, an atom can be compressed if there is enough gravity involved, making it much heavier for the amount of space taken up. Thus, blackholes and neutron stars can be relatively small yet have stronger gravity than Earth.

4. Can objects be moved or controlled by your thoughts alone?

Yes. Your entire body is electrical and your brain emits electrical impulses. Scientists and engineers today are learning how to use these brainwaves to control such things as prosthetic limbs i.e. artificial arms, legs, hands, etc. Control of some electronic devices is also being developed based on the same principle. Many people believe that "thoughts are things" which have a specific type of energy which can be harnessed. In this story this is the basis of holographix, which react based on a person's thoughts and feelings.

Chapters 18 - 19

1. The electroid or 'troid, Aggie, is an example of linear thinking. Why?

Most robotic devices are driven by computer code which progresses one line at a time. When it reaches a decision point then it will proceed through another set of commands. A computer can process information very quickly but it will typically do so one step at a time. Humans, however, can process information in a more holistic manner, comprehending many things at once and drawing from experience. Computer programs are limited to what they include. They cannot learn. A computer that can learn is known as "Artificial Intelligence." Computer scientists are beginning to develop such devices.

2. What are the specific steps you take to do something such as make a sandwich? Do you think of them as sequential steps or simply a single process?

3. Free will allows you to think whatever you want. Does that mean you can do anything you want?

4. Do you think it's possible to control other people's thoughts? Would this be good or bad?

5. Do you think that "thoughts become things?"

First, consider that nothing comes into existence without first being a thought. What power does a thought possess? How is it limited?

Chapters 20 - 23

1. Do you think you are right-brained or left-brained? Why?

2. Would an inclination to be right or left-brained be inherited or acquired from your environment?

While both have an influence, the inclination is mostly inherited, indicating the genes you possess from your parents and grandparents play an important role. These physical characteristics then contribute to how you think and behave even though this is where your environment also has a strong influence.

3. Do different cultures show more of a propensity for one or the other?

Yes. Some revere creativity while others discourage it. If you were born with a strong sense of creativity but in a culture that discouraged it, then it would never develop to its fullest capacity and you would probably be frustrated, even if you didn't understand why.

4. Sharra is gradually gaining courage and learning to make decisions. When she converses with Zahra she doesn't understand much of what she's told. Why not? Why do you think that Deven understands even though he's only a child?

Sharra's Miran roots discouraged creative thinking and making decisions. What Zahra tells her is based on intuition and abilities Sharra has not developed. However, Deven has inherited strong intuitive genes from his father and is young enough that Mira III hasn't influenced him that much, allowing him to grasp what she's saying. To some degree everyone is programmed a certain way, making it easier to comprehend some things better than others. This is why some people are better at spelling or math than others, because their brain operates differently. Learning something you are not naturally designed to do is possible but more difficult.

5. Is Creena acting like a typical Miran when she proposes they find or build a ship to leave Verdaris?

No, a typical Miran would probably sit and wait to be rescued regardless of what was going on around them.

6. Why is Creena nervous about the ship landing? Which information is logical or left-brained and which information is intuitive or right-brained?

The fact there's a ship coming to a planet where everyone has evacuated is unlikely and based on logic; the bad feeling she has is intuition.

7. Why would a "quantum paralysis device" be better than a refrigerator?

Because this fictitious device actually stops chemical reactions while a refrigerator simply slows them down since reactions occur more slowly in a colder environment.

8. What is "acoustical cooling?" How can sound waves make something colder?

Sound is a form of energy and energy is always conserved, meaning it cannot be destroyed or created. However, energy can be converted from one form to another. One measure of the amount of energy present is heat, which if used to create a different type of energy, such as sound, will be reduced and therefore cooled.

Chapters 24 - 26

1. How can a spacecraft use gravity to save power?

This is another example of converting one form of energy to another. A spacecraft can use the gravity of a planet which tends to pull it closer (centripetal or center-seeking force) to give it extra velocity. NASA interplanetary spacecraft use this method to speed up without having to use additional fuel. Most spacecraft exploring the solar system do not have propulsion systems. Rather they operate based on Newton's 1st Law which states that an object will remain in a state of rest or a state of constant velocity unless acted upon by an outside, unbalanced force.

A rocket is used to take it outside Earth's atmosphere and send it in a certain direction. The rocket is left behind and the spacecraft proceeds forward at the speed attained from the rocket. When the spacecraft gets near a planet, particularly a large one like Jupiter or Saturn, it is drawn toward it, speeding it up. If it is on the correct trajectory or path, it can use the gravity to sling it off in another direction or what is known as a hyperbolic orbit, which is an open arc, not a closed one which would put the spacecraft in orbit around the planet.

2. Why can't Aggie hear Thyron?

Thyron communicates through telepathy or brain waves, sometimes also called psi waves. Aggie's receivers are not naturally tuned to receive and interpret them. Not all humans can hear them, either, something that would also depend on heredity as well as the environment in which they were raised. Think about whether you have ever felt as if you could read someone else's mind or s/he could read yours. Was it truly telepathy or were you reading different indicators, such as body language and facial expressions?

3. What are Sharra's choices? Is there anything she hasn't thought of? What would you do?

Chapter 27 - 28

1. What skill is Dirck gradually developing from studying the ship's datalogs?

He's learning to tie seemingly unrelated facts together, a process known as synthesis. He's also becoming curious, something that was discouraged on his homeworld or *naterra*.

2. What effect could "transcription errors" have on a person?

Transcription errors are theoretical mistakes in reassembling a person's body based on their DNA coding after their body has been dissociated by a transfer beam or, in this case, the timebump experiences. Depending on which errors occur and the part of the body affected it could result in physical or mental disease, disabilities, or even death.

3. What would life on Earth be like if it orbited two stars in a figure-eight pattern like Cyraria?

The tilt of the Earth's axis is 23 degrees, which is what causes our existing seasons. The primary difference would be during the time when our planet was between the two stars, placing the entire planet in a "summer" mode that also lacked a diurnal cycle, i.e. night and day. In other words, it would be extremely hot with constant daylight. [NOTE:--This concept is explored in detail in volume II, "A Dark of Endless Days."]

Chapter 29 - 33

1. Think about the things you care about most and what it would be like if everything was suddenly gone. Would you accept the situation and give into your new circumstances or figure out how to get everything back? How?

2. Give an example of a time when you have used both logic and intuition to solve a problem.

3. Do you think Creena did the right thing insisting on going to Cyraria? Why or why not?

4. Have you ever known something without knowing why or how? For example, has someone ever called you and you knew who it was without even looking at the caller ID? What do you think it was?

Scientist, Dean Radin, has studied this phenomenon which was first noted by the famous psychologist, Carl Jung. Known as synchronocity, it implies humans have a sixth sense which can connect with others, particularly those with whom they have a strong emotional bond.

5. How much risk would you be willing to take for something you absolutely had to have? What kind of situation would it take for you to be that determined? Do you feel that way about anything now? Why or why not?

VOLUME II: A DARK OF ENDLESS DAYS

- Family dynamics: Parents make mistakes, too.

- Effects of orbital inclination on weather temperatures and patterns; planets other than Earth will be vastly different.

- Principles of self-sufficiency including water distillation and useful native plants.

- Engineering principles, e.g. how a heat exchanger (air conditioner) works using phase changes of the working fluid.

- Necessity of good planning coupled with back-up contingency plans.

- Consequences of using out-of-spec components and parts.

- Civil disobedience as it applies to political and personal freedom.

- Benefits of teamwork, structure and goal setting.

- Occam's Razor, i.e. the simplest solution is usually the best.

Chapter 1 (The Mother of Invention)

1. The title of this chapter derives from the expression "Necessity is the mother of invention." What are the true necessities of life? What are some of the challenges in attaining them? How do these challenges change based on location, weather and equipment available?

2. Indigenous people and primitive societies have lived everywhere from the Artic Circle to the equator for thousands of years. How do you think they coped with their respective environments? Think

about how they survived and with what, then take your list of necessities and divide it into necessities needed to sustain life, essentials that are important such as electrical power, and luxuries which you could probably live without, even if you didn't want to.

3. If you could, how would you change the weather where you live? How would that change impact the environment including plant and animal life as well as for humans?

4. Have you ever been in a situation where you didn't agree with what was being done yet found it difficult, if not impossible, to leave? Why?

5. What are some legal alternatives for getting something you need if you need something but don't have any money?

6. Most major projects encounter problems that require some sort of change. What do you do when you find yourself in that situation? Can you adapt easily and find creative solutions? Or do you get angry and give up? Which approach is most effective?

7. Why did the still remove the sediment from the water? When the water evaporated it left the sediment behind then condensed again as clear liquid.

8. Have you ever wanted or needed something badly enough that you tried to make or build it yourself?

9. Creative problem solving, sometimes called "thinking outside the box," is when you solve a problem in a different way by using your imagination and creativity to find the solution. Choose one of the challenges in your life and propose a creative way to solve it.

Chapter 2 (Wildlife)

1. What resources are available in your local area that would come in handy if you were a pioneer and first settler in the area?

2. Why do most areas of the Earth experience different seasons? The tilt of the Earth's axis, which always points in the same direction like a gyroscope. When it is pointing toward the Sun, the Northern Hemisphere experiences warm weather and the Southern has winter. When it's pointing away, the opposite is true.

3. Why does the Sun appear to move across the sky? The rotation of the Earth. The Sun doesn't move, at least from the viewpoint of within our solar system.

4. Why does the Sun's position change with the seasons? Unless you live on the Equator where the change is minimal, the Sun will be higher in the sky in summer and lower in winter. When it is higher in the sky its path across the sky is longer and thus you have longer days with the reverse true in winter. The angle striking the ground is different as well. When the Sun is high in the sky it will feel hotter than when it is lower. Thus, in the summer the Sun is high and hot plus it's up longer while in winter the Sun is low and cooler in addition to being up for a shorter time, resulting in cooler temperatures.

The Sun will rise and set in a different place depending on the season. On the equinox (approximately March 22 and September 23) the Sun rises in true East and sets in true West with night and day of equal length. The longest day of the year, known as the Summer Solstice, is usually right around June 21, with the shortest day or Winter Solstice, right around December 22. The Sun will always be in the same position for those events which many ancient civilizations knew and lined up their pyramids and various other structures so that they would line up with the Sun on one of those days.

5. What should you always do before exploring wild areas? Find out what hazards are in the area such a wild animals or poisonous plants. It is usually best to go with an experienced guide.

6. What is one way to store energy? A method everyone uses in one way or another is the battery. There are several different kinds, most

75

of which depend on chemical reactions to release their power, such as those used in toys and flashlights. Larger batteries are used in automobiles which also depend on chemical reactions but are recharged by the car's alternator where mechanical energy is converted to electrical. In the case of solar power, the light from the Sun is converted to electrical energy and likewise stored in batteries for later use.

According to the principle known as the conservation of energy, energy cannot be created or lost, only converted to a different form. One of the mysteries scientists are working on today involves Dark Energy which occupies the Universe. Albert Einstein's famous equation $E = mc^2$ tells us that matter is a form of energy [Energy = mass x speed of light squared]. This principle relates to the development of the atomic and hydrogen bombs as well as nuclear power which release the energy stored in matter. Matter, in turn, condenses from energy.

Chapter 3 (Confessions and Concessions)

1. What "secrets" do you have that you've never shared with your parents? Why? Does anyone else know? Could they use that information against you in some way? If someone were to observe your every move day after day what could they learn and possibly use against you?

2. Who would you go to if you needed help with something important? Why? What have you learned that you could share with someone younger or less experienced that would make their life easier?

3. Why do items cost what they do? What is the concept of "supply and demand?" The price of anything depends on several factors including the cost of materials, paying those who produce the item, expenses such as the equipment needed, and transporting it to the customers. This last expense is one of the reasons prices always go up with the price of gasoline. These are the costs related to what is known as the wholesale price or what a store or distributor will pay

plus a certain markup so the producer makes a profit. The store or retail outlet will also add a certain amount to the price so they, also, make a profit.

There is a saying about setting the price on something at "what the market will bear." This refers to how much customers are willing to pay for the item. If it's too low the seller could be making more money and may run out of the item. If it's too high, then no one will buy it and it will not make them any money at all or even indirectly cost them money if it is taking up space in their store where something more profitable could be placed. "Supply and demand" refers to having enough product available for everyone who wants to buy it. If something is in short supply then the price usually goes up. If there is too much then vendors will compete for customers and the price can go down. It will also usually go down if no one wants it.

Chapter 4 (HE/927-652-A)

1. What are the risks of going somewhere you've never been before, such as a foreign country, without learning something about it? There may be laws you're not aware of that you could break and get into trouble. If they speak a different language you may not be able to communicate with others. They may use a different type of money in denominations that are unfamiliar. Simple gestures you use all the time that don't mean anything bad could be rude or obscene in another country and cause a fight or even get you arrested.

The food may be extremely strange and consist of things you don't want to eat. The temperature there could be very different and require different clothing than what you usually wear. Sanitary conditions could be very different. There may be diseases there that do not exist in your native country which you could catch and become ill or even die. Transportation could be limited, expensive or nonexistent other than animals.

2. If you don't understand what's going on is it best to proceed or rethink your situation? Why?

3. What are some of the Earth's energy resources? As noted earlier, energy can be converted from one form to another. One example is hydroelectric power where the force of running water is used to turn turbines which in turn generate electricity. The water, in turn, obtains its power from gravity which results from the mass of the Earth. The Earth also has a massive magnetic field which results from the rotation of the planet's molten iron core. The Earth's magnetic field protects it from harsh radiation from the Sun and space itself by diverting it away. As yet science has not found a way to utilize this massive source of energy. Fossil fuel is another form of energy storage which is used to make gasoline and other petroleum products.

Chapter 5 & 6 (Worlds Apart & Earthbound)

1. If there's a conflict between what you think and what you feel which one do you choose? Why? Has that worked as expected in the past?

2. If you were Creena, who would you believe first, Thyron or Aggie? Why? Which do you trust more, logic or intuition?

3. Have you ever been treated unfairly? How did you react? Did it help or make the situation worse? Why?

Chapter 7 (Probability)

1. Have you ever had a friend who got you into trouble? Was it because it was wrong or because you simply didn't understand what you were getting into?

2. Why would anyone want to control your mind? To convince you to do what they want rather than allowing you to make your own decisions.

3. When you want or need something what is the first thing you do? If you can't afford to buy it then what?

4. Should you always be entirely honest, even if the information will make the other person sad or angry? Are there any exceptions?

5. What is probability? The term derives from whether or not it is probable or likely something will occur. This depends on how many choices or options there are. If you flip a coin there are two possible outcomes, heads or tails. Thus, you have one chance out of two that the one you choose will come up, also known as a 50:50 chance where $50 + 50$ adds up to 100% chance one or the other will occur. They say that lotteries are a tax on people who are bad at math because the chances of winning are usually one in a million or worse. Someone will probably win but the chance that it will be you is very remote.

Chapter 8 (Debits and Credits)

1. Is all truth logical? Is it possible to know something without knowing how or why it is true?

2. What's the connection between science and engineering? How are they different? Science studies nature and how it works. Biology is the study of life; geology is the study of the Earth; astronomy is the study of the stars and planets, and so forth. Scientists discover the secrets of these different subjects so we can understand the world around us. They develop theories and then set out to prove them, sometimes in the laboratory and sometimes through mathematical models.

Engineers take the information scientists provide and apply it to inventions that make life easier and more interesting. For example, Albert Einstein was a scientists whose theories were primarily math models, including one for the concept of lasers. It was several years before technology caught up to his ideas and was able to test them in the lab. Taking the knowledge provided by scientists and applying it to useful inventions and new technologies is the function of engineers.

3. Have you ever lost something that was valuable and/or meant a lot to you, perhaps because it was stolen? How did you feel about it?

4. What causes a tornado to form? A tornado forms from pressure differences related to temperature which are further fueled by the Earth's rotation which causes the air to rotate. A condition known as wind shear which relates to strong downdrafts is also a major factor. When cool air from one area collides with warm, moist air from another the mixing effect can spawn violent thunderstorms and tornadoes. The central part of the United States is particularly prone to these violent storm and known as "Tornado Alley." The terrain is mostly flat, allowing the air to build up energy more easily than it would in a mountainous area which would break up the air flow. Tornadoes tend to form mostly in the spring and fall when temperature differences can be dramatic.

Chapter 9 (The Lasomag)

1. If a law was passed you didn't agree with what would you do, especially if you felt you would be in danger as a result? Such a situation is known as a moral dilemma, where there is no easy answer and a downside to either choice. Reasoning can be sound for both, making the decision even more difficult with compromise seldom an option. Consequences associated with either choice are often harsh so careful consideration of all sides of the situation are required.

2. Has something bad ever happened to you or someone you know because you didn't listen to someone's warnings? What did you learn from the experience?

3. What are superstitions? Superstitions are usually beliefs that don't have a clear basis in scientific fact. Sometimes this only means that if there is any science involved it has not yet been discovered

and proven. They are often based on myths or unusual experiences that don't have any logical explanation. In many cases they have a basis in truth but cannot be explained in a rational manner. Some are silly, such as the practice of throwing a few grains of spilled salt over your left shoulder to prevent bad luck. Others, particularly those that relate to nature including the weather, may be based on observations of phenomena that cannot be explained at the time but may be proven later.

Chapter 10 (Colonel Jenkins)

1. Have you ever been in a situation where you didn't have the slightest clue what to do? How did you get through it? What would you do next time?

2. Is there any way you can really be prepared for anything? Practice, training and procedures can be useful for known situations, particularly those that are dangerous in some way. Experience with emergency situations helps you prepare for future ones of a similar nature. However, there are some events which have never happened before so there is no experience or precedent to draw from. In some cases, such a situation was never considered before. It's important to consider what emergencies have in common and have a basic plan for any of them. Knowing what to do when something goes wrong is the primary focus of individuals who go into the career field known as Emergency Management.

3. Who would you ask to help if you found yourself in a dangerous or difficult situation?

Chapters 11 - 13 (Friends and Foes, Pursuit & Escape)

1. What is *photosynthesis?* Photosynthesis is the process by which plants use light to generate the energy they need to grow. It is the opposite from humans in that they use carbon dioxide as part of the process and turn it into oxygen whereas people use oxygen when they breathe and exhale carbon dioxide. Thus, people and plants have a synergistic relationship is where each one produces

something the other needs to live. It is also sometimes referred to as the carbon cycle. Various manmade processes produce carbon dioxide that can upset this balance. It is known as a greenhouse gas because it tends to trap heat in the atmosphere and not allow it to escape into space. The planet, Venus, is a dramatic example of this effect with a thick atmosphere comprised largely of sulfuric acid (H_2SO_4) mixed with water and surface temperature of approximately 900 degrees. The greenhouse effect occurs when sunlight penetrates a planet's atmosphere as visible light then shifts wavelengths to infrared (heat) which cannot escape through the atmosphere to radiate off into space, thus continuing to heat the planet's surface.

2. What is meant by the term *reverse engineering?* In the simplest terms, this is the process of taking an object apart to figure out how and why it works, then trying to build another one. For example, if you took a watch apart you would see the components hidden within its case. If you could figure out what each one did you could conceivably use that information to create another one. However, if your knowledge of technology is not as advanced as the device you're taking apart you probably would not be able to figure out how and why it works and duplicate the process.

3. What is *culture shock?* Culture shock results when a person moves or visits somewhere that is entirely different than what is familiar to them. The behavior a person has learned, certain customs, traditions and even language including such things as slang and colloquial expressions are either ineffective or not understood in the new area, resulting in confusion and loss of security. Cultures operate on several levels and can comprise family or school traditions as well as that of a geographical area such as a city, state or country.

When immersed in a new cultural environment a person can either cling to their old norms of behavior or attempt to assimilate all or part of the new ones. In either case, a certain period of discomfort is likely as the individual unlearns some elements of their background, such as an accent that identifies them with a certain area, and adjusts to the new. The level of resistance to change, acceptance of the new culture, and pressure from those in the new area all contribute to the process which can take years or in some cases, never be achieved with the person the proverbial "fish out of water." For example, picture an Eskimo from the Arctic suddenly moving to Mexico or vice versa. While their physical appearance may not be that different, everything else about their cultures would be from their traditional dress to food and shelter.

Chapters 14 - 15 (Aftermath & Serendipity)

What is the best course of action when a person is overwhelmed and doesn't know what to do? Find someone to talk to who will calm them down and help figure out what needs to be done in a logical sequence.

Chapter 16 (The Bensons)

How many constellations can you identify? Do you know the myths associated with them? The stars look as if they are all the same distance away, as if a giant bowl were inverted overhead. This view is known as the Celestial Sphere which has specific markers so that astronomers can identify the location of the stars, planets, asteroids and other celestial bodies. The stars are extremely far away and even though they may appear to be close together in the sky, they are usually not. Some lights that appear to be stars are actually other galaxies, with 100 billion stars in the Milky Way Galaxy and 100 billion galaxies in the known universe.

The other planets in our solar system look somewhat like stars except they move more quickly, thus being called "wanderers" by ancient civilizations who didn't understand what they were. Since the star patterns remain the same they are often referred to as the Fixed Stars. A band of twelve constellations known as the Zodiac surround the Earth along what is known as the ecliptic or apparent path of the Sun and form a backdrop for the planets. You cannot see all of them at once and will only be visible certain times of year. Consider that the Earth goes around the Sun and night occurs when your side of the Earth is facing away from the Sun. Thus, the view of the night sky varies as the Earth orbits the Sun, always looking in a slightly different direction.

Chapter 17 (Cover-ups)

1. What is one of Earth's most well-known satellite networks? What does it do? The Global Positioning System or GPS, probably one of the most well-known satellite networks, provides you with position information. It is used for numerous applications from Facebook to locating stolen cars. There are 31 satellites, all in slightly different orbits at approximately 12,600 miles above the Earth. At least four satellites need to be above the horizon for a GPS receiver to calculate its location. This is done by computing the distance to each of the satellites based on the speed of light, i.e. the length of time it takes to receive each radio signal. These are then combined to determine the exact latitude, longitude and altitude. Other well-known satellites include the ones that deliver television programming, some internet providers and others used in telecommunications.

2. What is an eclipse? The two types of eclipses most often observed from Earth are solar and lunar. In a solar eclipse, the Moon passes between Earth and the Sun in a position where it blocks the Sun's light. In some cases it only blocks a portion of it, in others it may cover it completely or cover it with the exception of a ring of light which is called an annular eclipse. It's interesting that the Moon is the exact size needed to cover the Sun and thus cause a total eclipse.

However, the Moon's orbit is elliptical and is not always at the same distance. If an eclipse occurs when the Moon is farther away and thus smaller, it may not cover the Sun and thus result in an annular eclipse. Solar eclipses are only observable over a small region. A lunar eclipse occurs when the Earth is between the Sun and the Moon with the Moon passing through the Earth's shadow. They last much longer and are seen over a much larger area than a solar eclipse.

There are usually at least two of each type of eclipse each year, sometimes more. They occur when the Sun and Moon are within a

84

certain distance of the lunar nodes, which are where the Moon's orbit crosses the ecliptic or apparent path of the Sun. Ancient civilizations such as the Mayans studied eclipses and were able to predict them far into the future with amazing accuracy. Some cultures saw them as bad omens or indicators of something that would happen, often of an unfortunate nature.)

Chapter 18 (The PLED)

1. Have you ever been able to predict what someone would do? How did you do it? Do you think that you are predictable? If you know a person very well you usually know how they'll respond to certain situations. However, everyone has free will which means they can decide for themselves how they'll react and may not always be consistent.

2. What are the advantages and disadvantages of having information available about everything a person has ever done? It makes it more difficult for people to maintain their privacy. On the positive side, if someone is dishonest it's easy to find out but conversely dishonest people can also access the information and use it for illegal purposes such as what happens with identify theft.

Chapters 19 - 20 (Chores & Hauling Hay)

1. What is the purpose of chores? Chores teach responsibility as well as various skills. They also contribute to a sense of teamwork and working together for a common goal when used within groups or families to get things done.

2. How do different types of music affect you? Do you ever use it to create a mood such as cheer you up, induce relaxation or simple to have fun?

3. If you could create a planet what would it be like? What would you change about Earth if you could?

85

Chapter 21 (Return of the Cannibal)

How do you know when you can trust someone?

Chapters 22 - 23 (Prepare and Beware & Beneath the Surface)

1. Have you ever found something out you really didn't want to know? How did you handle it?

2. How does a heat exchanger or air conditioner work? An air conditioner is based on the scientific principle that when a fluid changes phases [gas, liquid, or solid] there is a change in its energy state. Some processes require energy and others release it. In an air conditioner a working fluid absorbs heat energy which causes it to evaporate or change phases from liquid to gas. The gas is then delivered to the condenser where it is cooled, usually by a fan, which releases the heat and returns it to the liquid state, further assured by the compressor for working fluids that would be a gas at normal temperatures, then begins the cycle again.

In other words, the heat is transferred from one location such as inside a house and delivered outside where it is released. Ice cools a drink in a similar manner. As it absorbs the heat in the liquid the ice melts, creating a phase change again as it goes from solid to liquid. Another everyday example is steam, which can induce a serious burn as it releases its energy and condenses to its liquid state.

3. Have you ever worked long and hard on a project until it was finished? How did you feel when it was completed?

Chapters 24 - 25 (Betrayed & Intrusions)

1. Has anyone ever lied to you then you found out later that they didn't mean to hurt you? How did you react?

2. Have you ever been tempted to do something you knew was wrong even though there were numerous reasons to go ahead and do it? How did you decide what to do? What were the consequences?

Chapters 26 - 27 (Beating the Heat & Opposition)

1. Has someone ever gotten something you really wanted such that you got jealous? How did you feel toward that person?

2. How effective is revenge? Who does it hurt the most?

3. Have you ever blamed someone else for a situation rather than accept responsibility or just deal with it? Does blaming someone else change the situation or make it better?

Chapter 28 (Departing)

 What is Creena's dilemma in this chapter? What are the pros and cons of her choices?

Chapter 29 (Surviving)

What is the best way to solve a big problem? Prevent it from happening in the first place. If this can't be done, remaining as calm as possible and gathering what resources you have is best.

- Creative problem solving, use of fault trees to cover project or engineering contingencies and real-time applications.

- Cavern formation and geology.

- Nonverbal communication including body and sign language, telepathy and psi ability.

- Metaphysical precepts such as veridical dreams and spiritual intervention.

- All is fair in love and war.

- Different cultural norms can clash with your own; indigenous cultures have a quiet wisdom lost in "advanced" civilizations.

- Properties of crystals such as birefringence and refraction.

- Political structures and differing ideologies.

- Risk of hasty conclusions and emotional reactions when all the facts aren't available.

Chapter 1 (Enoch)

1. What's the difference between a cave and a cavern? Caves are typically no more than a natural gap or hollow within a larger rock formation. The Earth is approximately 10% limestone which formed from marine shells when most of the planet was under water. Carbon dioxide in the soil is acidic and eats away the limestone to form calcite. There are many different kinds of water, depending on its acidity. Most common to everyday experience is fresh water, such as that found in most lakes and rivers, and salt water such as that found in the oceans and seas. Salt water has a lower oxygen content which is why animal life that can live in fresh water may not survive in the ocean. Salt water does not erode limestone. Sometimes the water in a cave can be hazardous and even comprise sulfuric acid

when hydrogen sulfide gas from deep in the Earth's crust bubbles up from oil deposits and is absorbed into the water. The sulfuric acid dissolves the limestone and forms gypsum, most commonly known as the substance in sheetrock which is commonly used for walls in building construction.

Caverns typically form when fresh water, often from rain, drips through limestone and dissolves it which can open up large underground areas as well as form stalactites and stalagmites. A stalactite is a vertical formation that starts overhead which is created as the water evaporates and leaves the limestone behind. It can be as fine as a needle or thick as a column and grows slowly with time, sometimes on the order of a millimeter over many years. A stalagmite is similar except it starts from the ground and works its way up. In may cases the stalagmite grows from water dripping from a stalactite and eventually the two will meet and form a column. It's easy to remember which is which because a stalactite starts at the ceiling and a stalagmite starts on the ground.

There are many caverns with these formations including Natural Bridges Caverns in the Texas Hill Country and Carlsbad Caverns in New Mexico. Some caverns are formed by underground rivers called aquifers which hollow out the rock in its path. These will typically have fewer stalactites and stalagmites but will show where whirlpools and eddies formed patterns in the rock along with other types of crystal formations. A typical cavern of this type is Longhorn Caverns between Marbles Falls and Burnet, Texas.

It is totally dark within a cavern which blocks all outside light once you are far enough from the entrance. Nonetheless various species will call a cavern home. Bats are typically associated with caverns. Since they are blind the darkness is irrelevant. They sleep in the cave or cavern by day and come out after sunset to catch insects. Caverns often have a dank, musty unpleasant odor which results from the bats' waste known as guano, which makes an excellent fertilizer. It's normal for thousands and even millions of bats to occupy a cavern. They typically hibernate in the winter. In some cases cockroaches who occupy the cave eat the guano and the bats,

89

in turn, eat the cockroaches, creating a synergistic life cycle between the two species.

Deer Cave in Borneo is so huge that the largest jumbo jet could fly through it. It is home to three millions bats. Certain species of birds also nest in caverns such as some swallows and cave swifters. Cave swifters in a cave in Borneo build their nests from their own saliva, which takes approximately a month to build. These nests are the main component of "birds' nest soup" which is considered a delicacy. Other species that can live in caves include huge centipedes, salamanders, crabs and fish. Without light they are blind. It takes thousands of generations for eyes to evolve yet it would only be a matter of weeks before you would go blind if confined to total darkness.

The activity of exploring caves is known as spelunking. There are many hazards involved and it should only be done with a properly trained and experienced guide. Exploring areas under water requires diving gear and is even more dangerous due to the possibility of becoming lost within hundreds of miles of passageways.

The temperature within a cave is usually within a small range due to being insulated by the surround earth and rock. Most Texas caves are around 68 degrees year round, making them a haven from summer's heat.

2.   Earth has diverse climates and environments yet most are occupied by human beings and have been for centuries. From extreme Arctic conditions to the desert, people adapt and survive. The most populated regions are mostly in what are known as the temperate zones where there are usually four seasons and moderate weather. Modern conveniences have made living in some of the harsher areas easier. Consider what it would be like to live in your own area without any technology. What about living in an area very different from what is familiar. How would you like living in an area like Alaska where the Sun barely shines in the winter yet hardly sets in the summer? What about somewhere like Central America where the temperature and weather is similar most of the year? Do

you like cold or hot weather better? What are the pros and cons of the different climates?

3. Unfamiliar cultures, people and races can seem strange and scary. Even within an area such as a single state there can be cultural differences. These usually evolve through necessity which eventually becomes tradition with the origin often long forgotten. Nonetheless, cultural norms or habits came about for a reason that may not be understood by those outside the group. Whatever culture you are raised within will seem normal with anything different from your own strange and unfamiliar. You may even think others are actually wrong. Moral judgments of a culture you do not know or understand can be unfair without knowing the practice's origin or rationale. The study of anthropology examines other cultures, their practices, language and civilization.

When a person leaves their own culture for another they can experience aa reaction known as culture shock. This can occur even when the differences are subtle, such as from one state in the USA to another. Accents, expressions, food traditions and clothing will differ, resulting in insecurities. When an entire group emigrates to a new country or environment it can result in culture clashes, where each thinks they are right and the other wrong. Learning to coexist with others different from yourself has challenged mankind for thousands of years.

What cultural differences result in problems where you live? What problems exist in the world today because of misunderstandings and intolerance?

4. Have you ever been in a situation where you were entirely dependent on someone else in order to survive? Were you comfortable with the situation? Why or why not?

5. What are some situations where you might have to take action based on instinct instead of knowledge or experience? Where do instincts come from? Some theories state that the memories of your ancestors are stored in their DNA and passed on to you. This is one

possible reason why birds know where to migrate and a potential explanation for various other animal behaviors. What useful skills might you have inherited from your parents or ancestors? Artistic talent, math or music ability, and physical traits are a few possibilities.

Chapter 2 (Visions)

1. Early psychological and psychiatric studies have addressed the source and meaning of dreams. Why do you dream? Have you ever had a dream that was a premonition of future events? Dream symbolism is unique and their meaning seldom obvious. Even colors have specific interpretations. Have you ever had the same dream more than once? This is called a recurring dream. What do you think it means? Why are dreams necessary?

2. Premonitions and psychic ability were once dismissed by science but are being studied today in an attempt to discover how they work and why. Scientists such as Dean Radin and several others study the human consciousness and its abilities that currently do not have any scientific explanation. While they have not identified how psychic phenomena operate they have done statistical studies that show when something goes beyond simple chance. Similar studies have been conducted regarding the practice of astrology by a scientist named Michel Gauquelin.

Many scientists reject these subjects and studies because they cannot be proven mathematically or by experiments which are repeatable. History has shown, however, that many of these subjects that were at one time rejected by mainstream science eventually were accepted as the evidence for such increased or technology developed which was able to detect such phenomena. Maintaining an open mind and investigating the evidence for such subjects is the best approach rather than making assumptions that may later prove false.

3. World history is filled with individuals and political forces that wanted to use or control others. Examples include Adolph Hitler, Joseph Stalin, Benito Mussolini, Napoleon, Attila the Hun, Genghis

Khan and the Holy Roman Empire to name a few. These entities initially gathered numerous supporters yet eventually failed. Consider what motivated those who wanted power and control as well as those who fought such efforts.

4. Have you ever had a strong impression to do or not to do something? Did you heed the warning? If not, what happened, if anything? If it were to happen again what would you do?

Chapter 3 (The Think Tank)

1. Information gathering takes place largely through our five senses, i.e. sight, hearing, touch, taste and smell. When any of those senses are impaired, such as someone who is blind or deaf, the other senses are sharpened to compensate as much as possible. Sight allows you to not only see the world around you but is key to skills such as reading and observing another person's expression and body language, offering another level of information beyond what they are saying.

How a person smells provides information as well, whether it is expensive perfume, an athlete after performing a physical feat such as a marathon, or the smell of garlic from their native diet. A handshake likewise tells you something about a person through your sense of touch, whether it is limp, cold and sweaty or firm and confident. Taste can bring pleasure or displeasure and provide information regarding whether or not food will taste good or is spoiled.

But what about other senses such as instincts or psychic phenomena? What are they? Does everyone have them with only a few accessing them? Or is it their imagination?

The collective consciousness is a term used to refer to the overall mental state of humankind, the cosmic soup of mental energy emitted by every living person on Earth at any given time. It's interesting to note that sometimes scientific discoveries occur simultaneously in two different locations involving two or more individuals. One example is the "discovery" of the mathematical technique known as calculus which was invented in England by Sir Isaac Newton (1642 - 1727) as well as a man in Germany named Gottfried Leibniz (1646 - 1716.) Social ideas and themes predominate different eras, imbuing them with a personality of their own.

In modern times a man named Roger Nelson has conducted experiments using random number generators which tend to change in character when significant events occur or are about to occur, indicating a change of energy, for example around September 11, 2001. The Web-bot is another experiment which collects keywords from the internet and can indicate what many individuals are thinking or talking about and has been used as a predictive tool for world events. These theories are controversial and not believed by everyone since they are yet to be conclusively proven. However, proving something of this nature is difficult due to the lack of a scientific theory that predicts not only the behavior but the mechanism through which it is conveyed.

The concept of the Think Tank in this story theorizes that a crystal with certain properties could possibly collect and amplify thought waves but this is pure science fiction speculation. Nonetheless, crystals have been an important element in communications since the invention of the first crystal radio.

2. Have you ever gotten to know someone who you initially thought was "weird?" It's natural to be drawn to people who are like you but they will not be able to stretch your horizons like those who are not. Fear of the unknown, including people who seem strange, is natural, but like most fear, worth the effort to overcome. In particular, consider those who are handicapped or different from you in a way such as mental or intellectual. One example is those with Down's Syndrome. There is a wide range of abilities covered by this genetic problem from those who can function almost as well as someone considered normal to those who have great difficulty with the simplest tasks. However, anyone who has ever known one of these individuals has recognized, they are nearly always happy. Their

limited awareness shields them from most of the troubles of the world, much as a small child is usually unaware, allowing them to entirely embrace the present and whatever they are doing. They are curious about simple, everyday happenings and can teach you to embrace the many things you have to be grateful for in your life. Volunteer work with various organizations who help these individuals can be very rewarding, such as helping with an activity such as the Special Olympics.

Another example is those with autism or a form of that condition known as Asperger's syndrome. Again, there is a huge range of this affliction from those who function within "normal" range to those who are entirely in a world of their own. Many have incredible abilities, particularly in math, music, art or language and an ability to synthesize information in an amazing way. They see the world through different eyes, yet it is the same world we all live in which makes it all the more interesting to see it in a different way.

Yet another example is those who have full mental capacities yet are handicapped physically, either because of a birth defect, disease or accident. These individuals will be much like you other than their physical disabilities. How they compensate for their limitations and view life can be very enlightening for those who take such a simple thing as taking a walk for granted.

Chapter 4 - 5 (Plans & The Fault Tree)

1. What do you worry about? It has been said that worry is a waste of perfectly good creativity. Humans can typically only think consciously of one thing at a time and if you're fretting about something that will exclude thinking about anything else. Much of worry concerns things which will never happen, which is the worst case of wasted energy. While it is always good to have common sense, take proper precautions and plan for life in general, worry in the form of fretting is generally unproductive. If nothing else, it distracts you from the positive side of things and how to achieve important goals. Optimism or thinking on the bright side of things is more productive and conducive to energy and enthusiasm that

95

being consumed by doom and gloom. In the book, *"Infinite Possibilities: The Art of Living Your Dreams,"* author Mike Dooley admonished his readers to not worry about "the cursed hows." He claims that focusing on your goals and what you want doesn't require lots of worrying with regard to how you'll get there. He promises that as you visualize where you want to go that ideas and guidance will come your way in the natural course of things which you simply have to follow like stepping stones. Maintaining a sense of wonder, hope, faith and a firm belief in yourself will naturally lead you to your destination.

2. Physicists today believe that there are numerous other dimensions besides the four we are aware of, in other words three dimensions of space and one of time. One dimension is represented by a single point, such as the period at the end of this sentence. Add a dimension and you have a line or flat plane of existence. With another dimension you can define a physical object you can hold in your hand. Time relates to where that object may be at any point in time.

Yet current theories such as the one known as String Theory, suggest there may be many others which we cannot see, yet are not far away. While these theories are often mind-boggling, pondering what they could mean is a good mental exercise for your imagination. Spiritual beliefs commonly testify of another dimension of existence and have for thousands of years. The fact that science is starting to catch up with what spiritual leaders have been saying all along is certainly food for thought.

3. What do you think it would be like to live on Mira III where everything is mostly under control? What would be the advantages and disadvantages of such a culture? Self-control is something to strive for, whatever your age happens to be. We can control our thoughts, if nothing else, but this is not always easy so it could be advantageous to have a little help. Learning to delay a response is possible but takes practice as well as discipline. Some people are naturally more patient than others. If you have a temper you may find yourself provoked to anger in a blinding flash of adrenaline that puts you immediately into fight or flight mode. This take a lot of

mental energy and practice to subdue and usually takes a lot more effort than counting to ten, though that is a good start. Think about what you would like to control better and consider whether you would like someone to do that for you or whether you prefer to make all your own decisions.

4. Building a fault tree is one time when thinking about everything that can go wrong is a positive thing. As part of planning it helps assure success as you specifically consider all possibilities and define a way to prevent, work around or deal with the situation. This is a technique that was used heavily at NASA to assure they didn't miss anything. Fault trees were used to identify potential hazards and how to control them, which were then documented on hazard reports.

In some cases there may not be a control in which case the risk has to be accepted yet avoided as much as possible. This was contributed to by the quality of the component which assured it was designed and manufactured to appropriate standards as well as its reliability, which was a probability measurement of how long it would last before it wore out and failed to function properly. Think of an item you're familiar with such as a bicycle, toaster, lawnmower or some other thing that has the potential to hurt you in some way then make a fault tree defining what those hazards are and what would cause them.

Chapter 6 (Prisoners)

1. Numerous people have been clinically dead then been revived by medical technology. These individuals typically describe similar experiences regarding what it was like while they were "dead" or out of their body. In fact, these are often called "out of body experiences" or OBEs. These experiences are particularly interesting within the context of various religious views regarding the spirit and life after death. Do you know anyone who has experienced an OBE? How do you feel about their story? Do you think what they experienced was real?

2. Do you have any special talents? A talent is usually described as something one person can do much better than others. In many cases this derives from the fact that the person loves a particular activity or subject and thus spends a lot of time practicing, such as in dance or a sport, and/or learning about it.

Thus, most talents are developed and result from a person's love of something. Some are born with an obvious and rare talent, such as the ability to play a musical instrument without ever having had any lessons or instruction but this is very unusual. Even those who are considered extremely talented in some area usually spend many hours practicing so just because you have a talent doesn't mean you won't have to work at it.

Chapter 7 (Release)

1. When you are afraid or nervous you experience various physical sensations. Sweating, shaking, brain fog or racing thoughts are just a few that occur when adrenaline surges through your bloodstream along with various other stress hormones. This reaction is essentially the same whether you are face to face with a rattlesnake or an algebra exam. The latter is a condition known as test anxiety and afflicts students of all intelligence levels.

Ironically a bad case of test anxiety is likely to compromise your performance. The first step is to identify the cause which is usually fear of failure which will result in bad consequences. However, it's unlikely that it's a matter of life and death. Self-help books on the subject are available which can help you understand why you are so intimidated by exams with counseling an option as well. Learning to control anxiety in situations that are not life-threatening can help you eventually learn to maintain control in those that are.

2. What is one way to prepare for a critical situation? Of course mental preparation is important but even more so is knowing what to do. Those who make a living in crisis situations such as policemen, firemen, Emergency Medical Technicians (EMTs), healthcare personnel and those in the military go through long

periods of training to prepare them for as many potential problems as possible.

With training many procedures become automatic in that they don't require conscious thought. These individuals can enter a "zone" where they respond according to their training and avoid fear or confusion with regard to what has to be done. This is the purpose behind fire drills as well. When something becomes routine and you know what to do in a given situation are less likely to panic. What are some situations you could train for? It might be helpful to interview someone such as an emergency responder and ask how they have learned to suppress their emotions and fulfill their responsibilities while under pressure.

3. Why do you think that doctors often will not treat their own family members? No matter how well-trained or competent a medical professional is suspending judgment, retaining objectivity and controlling emotional responses is more difficult when the patient is a person you care about. This can induce nervousness and impair decision making and thus compromise the ability to take appropriate action.

Chapter 8 (Complications)

Murphy's Law states "Anything that can go wrong will go wrong." Do you think this is true? How do worrying and negative thoughts influence your actions? What's the difference between worrying about something going wrong and planning for something to go wrong? Worry usually means that you're fearful about something, which can induce anxiety symptoms discussed above. This can compromise your ability to think clearly. When you have a plan you can feel confident that you can handle any contingency, maintain mental clarity and not waste energy or adrenaline. It has been said that worry is a waste of creative energy.

What does this mean? Many things people worry about never occur, thus it is often no more than a product of their imagination. It also has a negative spin that the outcome will be bad. Focusing on how to solve a problem restores a sense of control. Then you can develop procedures that you can train for and then respond in a logical, confident manner.

Chapter 9 (Waiting)

1. Why do you think medical technology failed to bring 'Merapa back to life? Why could Win bring him back?

He'd made up his mind he wasn't coming back. Win commanded him to come back at the spiritual level as opposed to the physical.

2. What do you do when you need the answer to an important question? Do you "rack your brain," research the issue, or find a quiet place to ponder what the answer could be? Which do you think is most effective? Why?

Chapter 10 (Recovery)

1. If you were a doctor with two patients of the same age and general physical condition with the same disease but one was unhappy and lonely and the other was happy and surrounded with people who loved him which one do you think would be most likely to get well? How does your mental state affect the way you feel physically? What do you do to cheer yourself up or do you count on other people to do that?

2. Name some things you know are real but don't yet have scientific explanations. Do you think that science will eventually uncover the reason for everything, including life itself?

3. Throughout history both science and religion have been right sometimes over the other as well as wrong. Sometimes religion turns a deaf ear to scientific theories which have been well-proven and science often ignores or vilifies phenomena it can't explain. What is the basis of their respective attitudes?

Chapters 11 - 12 (Politics and Alliances)

1. What does the expression "No mistakes, only detours" mean to you? How can it help you learn from experience and progress?

2. Another expression to ponder is "It's not what you know but who you know." What are the positive and negative results when this happens? How can you use that principle in a positive way? Is it wrong to advance yourself by calling in favors? Why or why not?

3. Is Governor Woeyel's philosophy of government liberal or conservative? What are the pros and cons of each?

4. Many of today's technologies originated as military applications. One example is the GPS (Global Positioning System) satellite network which originated for military surveillance activities and has now been released for civilian use. Even space exploration began with military motivations. When President Dwight Eisenhower created the National Aeronautics and Space Agency he wanted it to be a civilian agency, not one run by the military. Nonetheless, it was the Cold War back in the 1950s that motivated the United States to get to the Moon before the Russians. Why would the Moon make an important outpost?

5. If you could increase your knowledge and intelligence by simply entering a certain room what would be the first thing you would want to know?

Chapter 13 (The Miran Connection)

1. Have you ever been reunited with someone close to you from whom you'd been separated for a long time? What surprised you the most about the reunion?

2. Why is it important to maintain proper appearances and avoid situations that can be misinterpreted? Why is it risky to draw conclusions based on appearances alone?

Chapters 14 (Negative Spikes)

1. What can you tell about a person from what they read, watch on TV, or the games they play?

2. If thoughts become things what effect could good ones have on their surroundings? What about bad ones?

3. Have you ever tried to learn another language? What are some of the other ways that people communicate? Did you know that during World War II the Americans used Native Americans to communicate over the radio so that no one would understand their messages? The Navajo language was spoken only with no writing associated with it and limited to America, making it nearly impossible for foreign powers to learn the language or have access to it. Not all languages have a written component and some are not spoken, such as American Sign Language but they are all intended to allow communications.

4. Of similar interest is the Rosetta Stone which was discovered in the town of Rashid in the Nile Delta of Egypt in the year 1799. Literally a stone, it contained the text of a decree made by King Ptolemy V in 196 B.C. in three languages, the lowest form of ancient Greek, ancient Egyptian hieroglyphs and Demotic, which was a form of Egyptian used primarily for administrative and documentation purposes. Since the text was nearly identical and scholars were familiar with ancient Greek, it enabled them to understand Egyptian hieroglyphs and open the way to their translation.

In other words understanding an unfamiliar or foreign language requires a reference point whether it's an object to define the word or establishment of some other commonality. Some languages such as those known as the "romantic" languages which are those derived from Latin as the language of the Roman Empire have the same root. This applies to French, Italian, Spanish and Portuguese as well as some English and German words. They are often pronounced very differently but recognizable when written as having the same origins. For example cat (English), katze (German), and chat (French) all derived from the Latin version, cattus. The Rosetta Stone can be thought of as the antithesis of the Tower of Babel story in the Bible which describes the confusion of the prevailing language at the time into several different dialects, preventing the people from communicating with each other.

Chapter 15 (Delta-Sub-Q-Alpha-Prime)

1. What are some of the reasons that the habitable planets in an intergalactic society would employ space stations as points of entry? First of all, intergalactic spaceships would be extremely large and therefore heavy. In order to escape from a planet's surface into space requires that a vehicle go at least as fast as the planet's escape velocity which depends on its gravitational strength. Current technologies employ rockets which require a lot of fuel to acquire that speed which is why they are large and usually employ different stages which are left behind as the fuel is used up.

At the present time science has not determined how to neutralize gravity because they don't actually know how or why gravity works. Advanced civilizations on other planets, however, could have figured this out and employed it into their transportation. In that case, landing and leaving again would not be a problem. However, if a planet allowed all vehicles to land at will they could also be invaded by hostile forces. There is also the possibility of contamination from other worlds which could be lethal for its inhabitants, plants or animals. Thus, coming in through a central point provides greater control of both a social and health-related nature.

2. With the advent of advanced electronics robots have been developed which can perform a variety of tasks. They are used in manufacturing to perform routine and predictable tasks and can also be used as advanced instruments which allow human operators to do more than they could unassisted. Remote control via radio waves allows the operator to be at a substantial distance away, often to maintain a safe distance from hazardous environments. Robots are

limited, however, and cannot make decisions other than those that are programmed into them. People can think and synthesize information based on experience which allows them to make real-time decisions in situations they have not previously experienced. Artificial intelligence refers to the ability of a robot to think and draw conclusions and gather experience.

3. A common algorithm or sequence of commands in computer programming in that known as an "if-then" statement. It tells the robot or devise "if" this is true, "then" take a specific action. As an exercise thinking like a machine, try writing down all the necessary steps for performing a simple task such as making a sandwich or getting ready for school. The next time you play a computer game think about the commands operating in the background that direct the game to behave as it does. Better yet, write down an algorithm for one of the most common actions using "if-then" statements.

4. A "synchronous orbit" is one where an object such as a satellite is always over the same place as seen from the planet. Communication satellites, including those that provide television and internet services, are in such an orbit. Of course they are not standing still. Rather, the time it takes them to make one orbit is 24 hours, the same amount of time it takes for the Earth to complete one rotation. They are therefore moving at the same rate which makes the satellite appear to remain in the same location.

The amount of time it takes a satellite to complete one orbit depends only on how far it is above the Earth. Its size or mass does not matter. Thus, whether it's a space station or a small communications satellite it will be at the same distance which is approximately 22,300 miles (35,900 kilometers) above the Earth. A geosynchronous orbit is also known as a geostationary orbit. It is circular but the satellite will be perturbed by the Moon from time to time which will require adjustments at the ground station or adjustments to the orbit by onboard thrusters.

Chapter 16 (Bryl)

1. What are some of the advantages of international cooperation in scientific research? First of all, combining the knowledge of scientists who received their training in different locales creates a synergistic environment where additional discoveries can evolve. Intellectual and cultural diversity stimulate creative thinking and seeing the same phenomena through different eyes.

Secondly, if several countries cooperate in scientific endeavors it is less likely that one will advance faster than the others and thus achieve technological dominance which could ultimately result in war.

Thirdly, many scientific and engineering projects such as the International Space Station are expensive endeavors. When several countries work together with each contributing financially the combined resources allow the group effort to pursue larger projects than either could alone.

2. What are some of the pros and cons of consensus? When everyone agrees it's easier to focus on a single goal or target. Otherwise everyone could be going off in another direction, literally or figuratively, and compromise the group's objectives. However, if everyone always agrees creative problem solving can be inhibited or nonexistent. Worrying about always obtaining others' approval can squelch ideas before they have a chance to mature. Breakthroughs typically come from unconventional approaches so honoring individual and different opinions are important, too.

Chapter 17 (Intuition)

1. How much can emotions be trusted? What is the difference between emotions and intuition? Emotions are actually a physical response to some sort of stimulus, sometimes positive and sometimes negative. Depending on your personality, some people are more affected by emotion than others. Emotions can be joyful or painful and drive conclusions and decisions that are not always

factual. If a person feel threatened in some way then their sense of security is at risk which can activate the "fight or flight" response.

The important thing is to recognize when your thoughts have an emotional basis. Talking through your feelings with someone you trust can help put them in the proper perspective and help you avoid making bad decisions not based on fact. Intuition, on the other hand, derives from your subconscious instead of your emotions. There is a tremendous amount of information stored in that part of your brain that you cannot access.

For example, years ago they conducted an experiment where test subjects were placed in a room with a ceiling covered with acoustical tiles that had numerous holes in them. They were asked to count the holes and report their answer. Most people counted the holes in a few tiles then multiplied it by the number of tiles to get an estimate. Then they hypnotized the individuals who were then able to effortless tell them the exact number of holes. A similar experiment involved reading a newspaper where they were told to focus on one particular story, which they were asked about. In spite of only reading that one story, when they were hypnotized they were able to convey every story on that page of the paper in vast detail.

Thus, you are constantly picking up on all sorts of information at a level beyond your conscious mind. Hypnosis is one way for accessing your subconscious where all this information is stored. Sometimes your subconscious will process this information and draw a conclusion which it conveys in the form of intuition which will usually be correct. It is not always easy to distinguish between feelings based on emotion and a feeling evoked by something in your subconscious. Learning to tell the difference is important, however, since emotions are often an inaccurate representation of truth while your subconscious can be a powerful ally.

2. What is electromagnetic radiation? Electromagnetic radiation is the technical term for what we know as light. However, the visible spectrum is only part of the radiation included in this type of energy. Each color represents a different frequency and wavelength as well

as energy level. Not all radiation can be seen, however, like microwaves and radio waves. A microwave oven cooks food because the energy is converted to heat as it meets resistance.

Infrared radiation, also at the low end of the spectrum, is recognized as heat. You may also be familiar with how the world looks through infrared goggles, where everything has a green cast. On the other end of the visible spectrum is ultraviolet, which cannot be seen. It is a shorter wavelength and higher frequency which can cause damage to cells and is also responsible for such everyday things as sunburn. Sunscreen blocks these rays and thus protects your skin. Xrays such as those used by the medical profession are stronger still and can cause even more damage in large doses. After that come gamma rays, which are the most dangerous, and are emitted by the Sun. Fortunately for us, Earth's magnetic field and ozone layer protect us from them.

To understand why, remember that we're talking about electromagnetic radiation which derives from an electromagnetic field. Electricity and magnetism not only go together but are inseparable. The Earth's magnetic field is caused by the planet's iron core being rotated, which actually creates electricity. Rotating magnets are common in motors and electricity in turn creates a magnetic field. This is why power lines, particularly large transmission lines from power plants, can cause radio signal interference as their magnetic field disturbs them.

Light is made up of tiny particle-like units known as photons which have energy related to their wavelength. Photons originate at the atomic level and can also be absorbed in a similar manner. An influx of photons from the Sun is thus visible in the form of auroras at the North and South Poles. Their color results from their interaction at the atomic or molecular level with Earth's atmosphere and demonstrates their change from high energy gamma rays to lower energy emissions in the visible spectrum.

3. What is encryption? Encryption refers to scrambling a signal or message into a form that disguises it so that no one else can read or

understand it. Of course both parties, the sender and receiver, have to understand the encryption scheme so it can be translated. This is usually done mathematically using a technique known as a matrix. The letters and numbers are scrambled according to a certain pattern which the matrix can scramble and unscramble.

This is more sophisticated than a simple scheme such as assigning numbers to letters such as A is one, B is two, C is three, and so forth. The consistency in that method makes it easier to translate. With a matrix, however, the letters will not always have the same value and be impossible to decipher. Secret codes have been used throughout history using a variety of different mechanical devices that functioned similar to the matrix. In modern times, computer technology has facilitated a variety of techniques for encoding messages.

Chapter 18 - 19 (Grounded Out; Home)

What is serendipity? The definition of serendipity is to make fortunate and unexpected discoveries by accident or is sometimes also referred to as an unexpected delight. Recount any such experiences you've had such as meeting the right person at exactly the right time to help you with something or finding something in a lucky and surprising way.

Chapters 20 (Operations)

Have you ever started a project without fully understanding what was required to finish it? Did you get discouraged and quit or do what was required to reach your goal? Usually when you give up at some point you will regret it with it often impossible to go back and resume the endeavor. On the other hand, when you persevere and keep trying, regarding of how much effort it may take, you will learn new skills as well as patience which will help you throughout life. An optimistic "can-do" attitude is always helpful when tackling a difficult task. It's important to know your limitations, however, and not try to do something so far beyond your capabilities that you are doomed to failure from the start.

For example, if you want to compete in a marathon you need to train and prepare a long time in advance, perhaps with the assistance of a good coach or experienced runner. You would start out with the right equipment such as good shoes and shorter distances to build up your strength and endurance. Difficult mental or intellectual tasks should be approached in the same manner, one step at a time and drawing from the advice and experience of others who have already accomplished what you hope to achieve.

Chapter 21 (Intelligence)

1. What is "situational awareness?" Situational awareness is a term that refers to being vigilant regarding what is going on around you. It is a significant part of military training but also relevant in your life as well. One example is defensive driving, where you watch those around you on the road and anticipate what they might do which could cause a hazard along with what your response would be to avoid an accident.

Another example is traveling in a foreign country where there is a high incidence of theft so you keep close guard on your possessions. Being oblivious to your surroundings can be dangerous as well if you are hiking in an unfamiliar area, don't know what kinds of wildlife you may encounter, temperature variations, challenging terrain, and so forth. Give an example of a situation where knowing all the facts would be essential to your well-being in a defensive manner.

2. How is being aware of your surroundings helpful? The other side of situational awareness is using it in an offensive manner to your advantage. For example, if you wanted to go on vacation but had a limited budget, you could find out ways to get the most for your money. You could watch for the best price on transportation such as airfare as well as accommodations such as available hotels, hostels, bed and breakfast inns and so forth. Collecting coupons for discounts on meals, researching where to get the best food for the least money, talking to other people who had already been there or doing research on the web could also help you find the best values.

You could find out what activities in the area are available for free and plan a budget for souvenirs as well. Deciding where to go to college is another example where gathering information to guide your decisions will help assure a positive experience.

3. How much can you learn about other people by paying careful attention to what they do and say? How much can you tell from a person's appearance and behavior? What type of person do you feel drawn to versus repelled? Do you know why you react that way? They say "A tiger can't change its stripes" which means people don't change. Do you believe that is true?

Chapters 22 (Mind Games)

1. Are you a detail-oriented person or a "big picture" person? What are the advantages of each? What are the limitations? A detail-oriented person can find small flaws or inconsistencies in an item or project plan. However, they may become so caught-up in trying to make everything perfect or solve one specific problem that they lose sight of the goal or vary off-course.

A "big picture" person excels at visualizing the end result, setting long-term goals and defining the basic plan for achieving them. However, this person may miss important details and obstacles which could be avoided by proper planning, such as running out of money before it's complete. Thus, when they work together they have a better chance of success.

Which one are you? What experiences have you had that demonstrate the strengths and weaknesses?

2. When you want something do you try to do it all by yourself, expect someone else to do it for you or decide who you can partner with to help your or achieve it together? This is another situation where understanding your goal, what is needed to get there, and identifying any help you may require are essential for avoiding delays and frustration as well as assuring success. Usually the more you are willing to do yourself, the more likely you are to succeed.

Always expecting someone else to do the work or help you out will not only prevent you from learning important skills and lessons but will ultimately fail when there is no one there to turn to.

There's an old saying "If you want something done right then you need to do it yourself." While there are exceptions since some things are impossible to accomplish alone, being willing to do your part is an important factor in accomplishing what you want in all phases of life.

Chapter 23 - 24 (Covert Ops; Intentions)

1. Think of someone you know whom you consider to be stubborn and opinionated. Now think of someone you know who is patient and always willing to listen, looks first to the facts, and compromises when necessary in a reasonable manner. Which person do you think will be more successful in the long run? Why? Now rate yourself on a scale of 1 to 10 with 1 being willing to listen and 10 being confident that you are usually right. Think about making any adjustments required to optimize the chances that others will share information with you or respect your opinion.

2. Can you always control your reaction to information or certain situations? This is usually a high-order skill that takes years to achieve. When a person feels threatened physically, emotionally or intellectually, their first instinct is usually a "fight or flight" response. In a primitive society this tends to assure survival but in modern culture where so many different situations exist it is not always accurate or advisable. While it is difficult to learn to control an adrenaline rush, you can learn to control what you say in response. If certain situations arise frequently you can figure out in advance how to react and rehearse it, either alone or with someone else. This equates to training which, as noted earlier (Chapter 7, item 2) can make your reaction a planned one that becomes automatic and assures it's appropriate. Think about past situations where you "lost it" and how you would handle it if it occurred again as well as any you expect to face sooner or later. Practice your response until it feels comfortable.

111

Chapters 25 (Unveilings)

What are the two types of lies? There are lies of omission and lies of commission. Are lies of omission any better than those that are deliberate? What are some of the reasons that people withhold information? When is it justified? When is it not justified? What are some of the risks? How do you react when someone withholds information that you find out later? How does it affect your trust of that person? Sometimes it is easier not to tell something to a person than deal with their reaction. Often it is not a matter of what you tell a person so much as how. This is where tact comes in, the ability to say something in the most uncontroversial manner and avoid getting the other person upset. This particularly applies to criticism.

For example, someone else's behavior may be extremely irritating but you have to be around this person all the time. You want to tell them to quit doing whatever it is, yet don't know how so you keep quiet. However, the anger keeps building up and you feel as if one of these days you're going to lose it and explode. You need to talk to him or her before that happens but don't know how.

One technique which helps this type of communication is to use what is known as "I" messages instead of "you" messages. For example, if you say "I feel angry and put down when you talk to me that way," it is likely to have a better result than saying "You really make me mad when you act that way." When you start a statement with "you" it sounds more like an accusation which will trigger a defensive reaction. When you start with "I" and declare your feelings or own reaction you take responsibility for yourself and are more likely to invite the other person to examine their own behavior than be defensive.

Chapters 26 (The Learning Curve)

What is a "learning curve?" A "learning curve" refers to the time it takes before you fully absorb a concept or how to do a specific task in an easy, non-challenging manner. For example, when you first learned the alphabet and then how to read you went through a period of time when you had to think about it consciously then gradually it became familiar and easy. This also applies to learning math facts, how to play a game or sport as well as any new skill. Are you ever afraid that you can't ever learn how to do something? Have you ever admired someone for their abilities and wished you had them yet doubted you could ever do so?

It's important to realize that unless someone is a blatant genius, which is rare, that they learned one step at a time and went through various levels of the "learning curve" before becoming proficient and eventually an expert. Think of something you currently wish you could do. Research what training would be required to do so and approximately how long it would take. If you know someone who is already proficient, talk to them and find out how long it took for them to get to that level.

Remember that the desire to do something is often the most important factor. If you want something badly enough you will have the drive and patience to learn, study and practice until you reach your goal, whether it's playing a sport or musical instrument or achieving excellence in a particular field of study such as science.

Chapter 27 (Questions and Answers)

1. How well do you accept being wrong about something? Do you argue and deny it, refusing to accept it, or logically examine the facts to determine the truth? How much does your emotional reaction hamper discovering and rectifying any mistakes? The ability to accept being wrong without feeling stupid or incompetent is important to success because everyone is wrong sometimes. Accepting it, being willing to listen and learn, then moving on smarter than before is how you progress in life. Those who never acquire the humility required to admit they are wrong can easily get stuck in various parts of life.

2. Have you ever been pressured into making a promise you couldn't keep? What happened? What lesson(s) did you learn?

113

Chapter 28 - 29 (Confessions; Treachery)

1. Have you ever been in a situation where you received "too much information?" Are there times when it's better to not know everything another person is thinking? Why do people withhold information? When is it detrimental? What kind of mistakes can be made when you don't know all the facts in a situation?

2. Are all laws favorable for the average person? Do they always protect people or can they have the opposite effect? What influences affect the making of a law and its enforcement? In the USA large corporations and special interest groups maintain lobbyists in Washington, D.C. to influence laws and regulations. What are some of the pros and cons of such a system? Do you agree they should have an influence or should all laws be based strictly upon what the majority of people want?

3. What causes an eclipse? There are two times every year when eclipses occur but they are not visible everywhere, particularly solar eclipses which are only visible over a narrow path. A solar eclipse occurs when the Moon moves directly in front of the Sun during its New Moon phase and casts its shadow on the Earth below. This does not occur every month because they only line up when the Sun is close to the lunar nodes or where the Moon's orbit crosses the Sun's path, also known as the ecliptic. Lunar eclipses occur when the Moon passes through the Earth's shadow at the Full Moon phase. These are visible over a much larger area since the shadow of the Earth is much larger than that of the Moon. Ancient people believed that eclipses were indicators of ominous events to come. Just for fun, the next time one occurs pay attention to whether something important occurs around that same time.

4. Have you ever missed an important fact? What were the consequences? Usually missing something important occurs when you are distracted in some way. Emotions especially can cloud your thinking and judgment. Remember the importance of knowing the difference between emotions and intuition (see Chapter 17, number 1 above).

Chapter 30 (Disaster)

Define "perseverance." Why is it useful? Perseverance is an important trait which relates to never giving up. Obstacles and difficulties are to be expected in pursuing any goal, which would never be obtained if you gave up too soon. However, is it ever time to quit, particularly if you are "beating a dead horse?" How do you know whether you should steel yourself with determination and continue forward or recognize you're wasting your time and cut your losses? When something reaches that point it is important to recognize all you have learned from the experience, even if you didn't wind up where you had hoped. Skills, lessons, connections and experience can always be applied to the next endeavor.

Recognizing why the effort failed is important as well so you can learn from it and avoid the same mistakes the next time. Those who have been successful always have numerous failures behind them which are often invisible to those who only see the present. Inventors have a strong appreciation of failures which help them determine how to improve their device. Any effort that turns into a major flop has value as a learning experience, particularly when you learn vicariously from the mistakes of others.

VOLUME IV: REFRACTIONS OF FROZEN TIME

- What motivates research
- Importance of innovation
- Perseverance in the face of difficulties
- Benefits of thinking "outside the box"
- Complexities of personal relationships
- Dealing with loss and grief
- Importance of optimism
- Relationship between thoughts, feelings and emotions

Prologue

1. What would you do if you really wanted to know something? Are you willing to research it, even if it's difficult or boring? Why is it important to be able to persist if uncovering information essential to a situation?

2. What are some professions where research abilities are important? Science of all varieties, forensics for criminal investigations, law interpretation.

Chapter 1 (Answers)

1. Why is electrical power important? We depend on electricity to maintain a civilized and advanced lifestyle. Nearly everything you do all day involves electricity in some way, whether it comes from an electrical outlet or a battery. Name some things you could no longer do if all of a sudden there was no electricity.

2. How is electrical power generated? There are several ways to generate electricity but they all ultimately involve a process that

results in a flow of electrons. The challenge is how to get them to move. Metals tend to lose electrons more easily than other materials which makes them good electrical conductors. Metals are also maleable, i.e. flexible, as opposed to crystals which tend to break. This all relates to how the atoms are bonded to one another.

Electrons are part of atoms along with protons and neutrons. The original model of the atom with which many people are most familiar is the one that looks like a mini-solar system with the protons and neutrons clustered in the middle and the electrons orbiting around it. While electrons have mass, they are part of the weird world of quantum mechanics and aren't necessarily a discrete particle but more often part of an energy cloud. Their charge is negative while protons have a positive charge and neutrons, as the name implies, are neutral. In their natural state, atoms have an equal number of protons and electrons so their charge is neutral. However, if an atom loses or gains an electron, then its charge becomes positive or negative, respectively, and the atom becomes an ion. It will then be attracted to other atoms with the opposite charge and repelled by those with the same charge.

You have seen this happen on a cold day when you get zapped touching something metal, such as a doorknob. Likewise when it's cold and dry and your hair is full of static. In this case, your hair stands up and out because it is no longer in a neutral state. But the electrons are not moving, which is why it's called static electricity. If one hair has the same net charge as the others, they will repel each other.

Sound familiar? Right. It's the same behavior as the response between like poles of a magnet. And guess what? There's a strong reciprocal relationship between electricity and magnetism. It's complex and scientists have only unraveled a small portion of the secrets they contain. But one thing we do know is that we can use electricity to create a magnet and we can use rotating magnets to create electricity. Light, the official name of which is electro-magnetic radiation, is also related. Some have achieved small-scale levitation with magnets and research is ongoing in this fascinating field of study.

3. What are "fuel cells?" Fuel cells generate electricity by combining hydrogen and oxygen which produces water, heat and orphaned electrons which provide an electrical current.

4. Why is it important for electrical wire to be insulated? Otherwise if you touch it you can be electrocuted.

5. What is a semi-conductor? A conductor carries electrical current while an insulator doesn't. A semi-conductor has properties of both which provides more options in manipulating electricity such as that used in electronic devices.

6. How can light influence electricity? Albert Einstein received the Nobel Prize for his work on the "photoelectric effect." Light is energy and comprises a particle known as a photon which can stimulate the electrons in an atom to a higher level or sometimes even cause one to be stripped off, changing the atom's charge from neutral to negative or positive, depending on what it's natural state is.

Chapter 2 (Transitions)

1. Why does Dirck think that false hopes are better than none? When all hope is lost, a person would be more inclined to give up. Even if what is hoped for doesn't occur, it buys time and something else could come along to help instead.

2. Laren Brightstar is a "terralogist" or planetary engineer. His expertise was converting planets that had the basic characteristics needed to sustain life, like an atmosphere and liquid water, into habitable domains. He ponders how tomography could manipulate weather and provide information regarding what was beneath a planet's surface, which was important for changing a planet as required to sustain life. However, the military and aggressive

entities such as the Integrator could also use this capability in a devious way. What are some of the things they could do? Create weather disturbances, droughts, floods, and massive storms or earthquakes in enemy territory which would give them a tactical and strategic advantage.

Chapter 3 (Departing)

1. What were some of the reasons that Dirck and Creena didn't get along? He was intimidated by her because she thought differently than he did and made him feel stupid.

2. Why was Dirck so impressed with Apoca Canyon? He was surprised it was so sophisticated and massive in contrast to how they'd been operating with old equipment out of the Caverns. He was also impressed that his father had been so involved in its development and the amount of respect he was given by everyone there. It is often difficult for children to see their parents as others do.

2. Why would TBAs (Technical Breakthrough Advisories) be issued? Who would receive them? Why? Most research projects are being pursued with a definite goal and purpose in mind which is being funded by someone. Thus, reporting progress is important to the person paying the bills to make sure that things are progressing as they should. They can also be important for determined whether or not a project is on schedule, which also has financial implications because paying people their salaries is often one of the biggest expenses in such an endeavor.

Chapter 4 (Apoca Canyon)

1. Why is Dirck surprised that the "Intelligence Processing and Synthesis" group was less effective than he and Win had been? They had more people and more sophisticated equipment but lacked leadership and procedures that flushed out the information.

119

2. Why is it important to deal with emotional situations rather than suppress them? Because they can be a distraction and cause additional problems such as poor judgment.

Chapter 5 (Psicom)

1. Deven has a knack for coming up with ideas, information, and in this case, a new crystal, that has tremendous promise for Creena's research. Why is this ironic? Deven usually makes such discoveries when he's doing something or going somewhere that he shouldn't. Yet, the family probably wouldn't be alive if it weren't for his exploits and what he learns.

2. What do you think of Deven's idea that it doesn't matter how something works, only that it does? What are the pros and cons of this approach? Pro: Discovering how something works could be revealed by experiments related to its properties and behavior. Con: Without understanding exactly why something behaves the way it does you could inadvertently create or encounter dangerous unexpected effects. For example, early experimentation with radium by the Curies resulted in them eventually getting cancer from the radiation exposure they suffered, which they didn't realize was dangerous.

3. Would you like to have the ability to communicate telepathically? Why or why not?

4. How would you feel about someone being able to read your thoughts?

Chapter 6 (Devenite)

1. Have you ever been around someone where you could feel what they were feeling, such as anger or love?

2. What are the advantages of being able to feel someone else's emotions? What are the disadvantages? Feeling another's emotions,

which is called empathy, can help promote understanding. However, there are times when a person is reacting in an inappropriate way which they will eventually get under control and change. Being privy to them before they're processed could actually cause additional misunderstandings.

Chapter 7 (A Knick of Time)

1. What do you think it would be like on a blackhole where gravity is so strong that atoms collapse? Are you aware of how much empty space is inside of an atom?

2. When Creena, her mother, Deven, Aggie and Thyron left the caverns, where did the psitenna combined with the Think Tank take them? Universal Time where the past, present and future are all mixed together.

3. Could there be such a place? Einstein's Theory of Special Relativity tell us that time is relative and changes near the speed of light or in a gravitational field. What do you think that time actually is?

4. Why does Laren think that time won't exist in either of his possible destinations? It's likely that time does not exist on a blackhole or when a person is dead.

Chapter 8 (Purple Haze)

1. Why do extreme temperatures affect electronic devices? Semiconductors are inhibited by cold while conductors are more efficient, which changes how they operate.

2. Dirck's feelings toward Creena have started to change. Why? He's beginning to realize how much he misjudged her.

3. How would you feel is someone gave you an assignment or project that you felt was entirely beyond your ability? Would you refuse or accept the challenge?

Chapter 9 (Vortices)

1. Do you ever feel as if you never do anything right the first time? What do you think of the saying "Good decisions come from experience and experience comes from bad decision?" Do you think that making mistakes is a part of life that you're supposed to learn from? Is this a good or bad way to learn? Why or why not?

2. Laren thinks that finances are "seldom a driver for a dictatorship." Why? Dictators can muster free labor from their populace which saves money in wages and salaries and they can direct what resources they have in whatever direction they choose without any input or protest from their citizenry.

3. Why did Rhodus' demand for an audit and recount for the election that brought Integration to his territory get him arrested? Integrated leadership didn't want everyone to know that they'd cheated to obtain power of the territory.

Chapter 10 (Many Happy Returns)

1. What finally motivated Dirck to solve the turbine problem once and for all? Why did he succeed this time when previously he had no idea what to do? He accepted the others were gone and decided that he would honor their memory by doing something to help the cause they cared about. Stress and grief fog the thought process so when he got past his emotional turmoil he was able to finally think clearly and find the solution.

2. Which trait of Creena's did Dirck change his mind about? That she refused to give up when she was committed to something, in this case bringing back their father.

Chapter 11 (R&D)

1. R&D stands for "research" and "development." How are the two related? Before a new technology can be developed, it needs to be researched and thoroughly understood.

2. The most expensive part of any endeavor can be the research phase. Why? It's difficult if not impossible to predict how long it will take to make a scientific breakthrough. Meanwhile, scientists and engineers need to be paid for their services while their sponsor isn't receiving any income from their efforts. This is why something that may seem like a relatively inexpensive device as far as its parts are concerned may be expensive as the company tries to make up for its investment developing it.

3. What are the advantages of using a table to record what you know or don't know about something? It helps you organize your thoughts and recognize what you know and what you don't. It also helps you set goals and define the tasks which need to be done.

4. What is "synergy?" Synergy refers to the ability derived from two or more substances which none could achieve individually. It can relate to people working together as a team or physical or chemical substances.

5. How do you think telepathy and other psychic phenomena work?

Scientist, Dean Radin, PhD, has done a substantial amount of work on these subjects which he has reported in his books "The Conscious Universe" and "Entangled Minds."

While science still cannot explain exactly how it works, they are beginning to finally accept it along with other paranormal phenomena as worthy of legitimate research. In what may appear to be psi, much progress has been made toward such devices as prosthetic limbs (artificial arms, hands, legs, etc.) which are operated seemingly by the user's thoughts while they are actually driven by electrical impulses to their muscles driven by their brain and consciously thinking about making the device respond.

Chapter 12 (Discoveries)

1. Have you ever been in a situation where you had to do something, even if it was wrong? How did you decide what to do?

2. Why did it get warmer as Deven went deeper into the cavern? Geothermal energy, possibly the planet's molten core heating the aquifers, i.e. underground rivers.

3. What is Deven's most important trait? Optimism. He always sees the positive side of any situation and believes that unfortunate ones will turn around. He never stops believing in a favorable outcome. It has been said that pessimists (those who always expect the worst) are more realistic than optimists, but optimists ultimately accomplish more. Why do you think that's the case?

Chapter 13 (Contact)

Why is it important that Creena, Dirck and Win figure out the communication abilities of the crystals before the Integrator does? If the Integrator solves the problem first they will use those capabilities against them. Whichever side has them first is nearly assured of victory.

Chapter 14 (Ethics)

1. Why did Laren tell them to abandon the crystal research related to time travel? He considered it immoral.

2. Why didn't Laren tell them what he was trying to do onboard the *Bezarna Express*? He wasn't entirely sure their conversation wasn't being monitored and he didn't want them to get their hopes up in case his efforts failed.

3. Troy and Spoigan have entirely different opinions regarding the incident where several test subjects were killed by Integration's research. Which claim do you think is more valid, that people are important resources or that the trouble makers will be too much of a problem? Why? Is there a compromise that incorporates both arguments?

4. What is the advantage of having opposing views? Seeing a problem from different sides fully defines the issue which often helps find the best solution.

Chapter 15 (Connecting)

1. What do you think of the concept of connecting with some people mentally and others emotionally? Paul Pearsall, M.D. is a cardiology who has written a book entitled "The Heart's Code" based on his experience with heart transplant patients. There were numerous instances where the recipient mysteriously acquired memories of the donor, particularly such things as favorite foods. Do you think there are some things you remember with your brain and others with your heart? What type of memories would you store in your heart?

2. Would you like to have a c-com? Which feature would you like the most? Do you think that "smart phones" will eventually evolve to have the same capabilities?

Chapter 16 (News)

Have you ever tried to protect someone's feelings by not telling them something they really needed to know? How did it turn out? Why is it difficult to give a person unfortunate news? Is it to protect them or because you fear dealing with their reaction?

Chapter 17 (Orders)

Have you ever been in a position where you had conflicting directives from two people? How did you decide what to do? Sometimes it's a matter of deciding which one needs to be done immediately and which one can wait but other times it's like one person telling you to turn left at the stop sign while another tells you to go right. How do you solve the dilemma?

Chapter 18 (Motives)

1. Do you think Sharra's suspicions are accurate? Have you ever suspected someone of doing something that turned out to be untrue? Did your incorrect thoughts cause any problems which could have been avoided if you'd discussed the matter with the person involved?

2. Why is Spoigan so intrigued by Antara? She is not intimidated by him.

3. Do you think that Antara did the right thing by making her c-com disappear? Or could it cause additional problems? What would you have done?

Chapter 19 (A Matter of Time)

Have you ever misunderstood a concept which resulted in coming to an incorrect conclusion? It's also easy to make mistakes and miscalculations. Even computers can make mistakes if they're programmed incorrectly. What mistakes have you made because you didn't understand something?

Chapter 20 (Waves)

1. How do you think devenite would react to negative energy? Would it respond to a person's intent if it were selfish or would harm another person? Or would it take them back to the point where the

negative energy originated and give the person an opportunity to see things differently?

2. Sharra has a dilemma. She wants her bondling back. Yet, if he returns, she's afraid she'll have to share him with Bryl. How (if at all) could she resolve the situation?

3. Scientist Roger Nelson has conducted experiments using a random number generator (RNG), a device that does as its name implies, i.e. picking numbers at random. He has these devices placed in various cities where they are monitored. When an event occurs which affects a large number of people, the random character of the numbers changes. Before the World Trade Center Twin Towers were attacked on September 11, 2001, the RNGs indicated something was going to happen even before it occurred. The RNGs also registered effects for such things as a sports event held in a massive stadium. What do you think the RNGs are picking up?

Chapter 21 (A Bit of a Break)

Aggie stated that the c-com was "a communication device that operates by connecting and synching with the encephalographic glial cells of the brain via quantum photon entanglement." This concept has been explored scientifically as part of quantum theory and states that when a photon is split the parts are nonetheless forever tied together.

Thus, when something affects one of the parts, all of the others are likewise influenced. Communication occurs instantaneously between them, i.e. faster than the speed of light, which suggests time does not exist. Dean Radin, PhD (mentioned previously in the questions for Chapter 11) has found this to be the case for psychic phenomena as well. When science figures out how this works, what do you think is one application it could be used for besides communicating with other people?

Chapter 22 (Actions)

"Action Items" are often assigned at meetings like the ones I attended when I worked for NASA. They consist of a specific assignment given to a person with a deadline as well as instruction regarding to whom they should report the information. Keeping track of actions as well as when they're completed holds the assignees accountable.

This relates indirectly to whether or not a person is dependable. How many times have you been let down by someone you counted on to help? How many times have you let someone down by not doing what you were expected to do? Why is being a reliable person important?

Chapter 23 - 24 (Customer Service and Charging)

1. Bernie and Antara communicate in code which comprises certain phrases which sound one way but mean something entirely different. Have you ever been in a situation where you used some form of a code? What other means of communication can convey a message without saying it directly? Body language and your facial expression are two of the obvious ones, but if you didn't want someone to know what you were saying what are some other means to do so? Would it require making arrangements beforehand for the person to understand or not?

2. Why do you think Spoigan was bothered by Friar Johann's prayer? Do you think he felt guilty for his intent or was more worried about his own well-being?

Chapter 25 (Intrusions)

1. Why do you think Sharra was defensive about Zahra's message?

She was worried they might not believe her or think she was foolish.

2. What does it mean, "Sometimes it's easier to get forgiveness than permission?" Doing something you're not supposed to for a good reason may result in not being in trouble with whomever you defied.

Chapter 26 (Brain Storms)

1. The world has less and less privacy due to the development of electronic surveillance. This applies to devices such as computers and cell phones as well as actual observing using such things as drones which in some cases can mimic the appearance of a flying insect. Is this a good or bad thing? What are the pros and cons of knowing what people are doing?

2. Many believe that "thoughts become things." This can be viewed in two ways. First of all, before you accomplish anything it starts with a thought followed by action.

The other way that it's interpreted is that a thought has metaphysical powers. The philosopher Johann von Goethe stated: *"Until one is committed, there is hesitancy, the chance to draw back, always ineffectiveness. Concerning all acts of initiative (and creation), there is one elementary truth, the ignorance of which kills countless ideas and splendid plans: that the moment one definitely commits oneself, then providence moves, too. All sorts of things occur to help one that would never otherwise have occurred. A whole stream of events issues from the decision, raising in one's favor all manner of unforeseen incidents and meetings and material assistance, which no man could have dreamed would have come his way. Whatever you do, or dream you can, begin it. Boldness has genius, power and magic in it. Begin it now."*

What dream would you like to come true?

Chapter 27 (Anticipation)

1. Your subconscious is aware of numerous things your conscious mind misses. Hypnosis is one way to access your subconscious

which is sometimes used so people can remember something they have forgotten or perhaps wasn't aware of at the time it occurred. You can tell your subconscious to help you solve a problem when you go to sleep and the next day it's likely you'll find the solution. Why do you think your subconscious is so powerful? Is it a part of your brain or something else? Do you think your consciousness is strictly linked to your physical body? Why or why not?

2. What would it be like to interact with an intelligent alien species? In this chapter you get a glimpse inside Igni and learn a few things you didn't before. What would the world be like if each community or even city operated like a colony of ants?

3. What are some of the qualities of Igni's culture? Lack of competition in favor of teamwork; Merging thoughts, ideas and ambitions into a single consciousness; No individual was expected to do anything alone; Swarming to assist anyone in trouble; Telepathic communications to name a few.

Chapter 28 (Ascending)

1. Why did the Quadrumvirate question Troy about his knowledge regarding Spoigan's visit to Esheron? They needed to determine if he was involved in any way with his death.

2. The "truth disk" used to determine whether or not he was telling the truth is a more advanced version of a lie detector which monitors a person's physical reactions to discern whether or not they are lying. How do you feel when you don't tell the truth? Are there some people you can never fool with a lie? How do you think they can tell?

Chapter 29 (Light and Dark)

1. Have you ever been in a situation where you thought you might die? What was your first thought? Were you at peace or terrified?

2.   One thing that technology attempts to do is increase our knowledge and comfort levels. The nanobots in the chairs described in the Star Trails Tetralogy stories sense a person's tension and then give them targeted massage and trigger point therapy to relax the muscles. A long time ago recliner chairs used to vibrate attempting to do the same thing but they were noisy and ineffective. How do you think they might work with nanobots?   Nanobots are microscopic size devices which can be programmed. Considering that your muscles operate with electrical signals from your brain, what do you think the nanobots might do to tell a muscle to relax?

Chapter 30 (Negativity)

1. What would you think if you were driving a car or piloting an airplane and it suddenly took off in a direction other than where you intended it to go? Would you panic? Someday automobiles may be under the control of some government agency where you program in your destination like you do now with a GPS but instead of driving there yourself, your vehicle would automatically go there? What are the pros and cons of such a system? Pros: Would help avoid collisions and other types of accidents; Individual driver abilities would no longer be an issue in traffic safety as well as distractions. You could sit back, do what you want and enjoy the ride; You wouldn't have to worry about getting to your destination, getting lost, etc. Cons: If there were any bugs in the system it could be even worse than current traffic issues; If the government wanted you to be somewhere it could take you there whether or not you wanted to go; Knowing where you are and how you got there would be compromised.

2. If you have a cell phone are you aware of everything it is capable of doing? How long did it take you to figure out how to do everything you wanted? How many things do you think it can do that you haven't yet discovered? Spend some time exploring its functions and see what handy new app you can find.

3. What do you think of Deven's insistence that having good on their side is enough? Do you think there are good and bad energies in the Universe? Can you sense when something is good or bad in a moral sense? Do you think that perhaps your conscience is driven by this energy?

Chapter 31 (Attitude)

1. What do you think Deven discovered about Cranium Cavern? What were its walls reflecting back? Why does he think the others have to experience it like he did or they might not believe him?

2. Do you think Bryl was justified not telling everyone of the plans she was putting in place? Is it always good for everyone to know all the facts? Or is leadership sometimes justified in planning for emergencies? Would you panic if you found out something bad was going to happen? What would make you feel better about confronting such a situation?

Chapter 32 (Karma)

1. When you are scared or upset can you think clearly? Most people cannot, mostly due to a blast of adrenaline in their system which promotes the "fight or flight" reaction to an emergency. Why would this affect your reasoning? All your energy needs to be directed toward dealing with the immediate situation. It's past the time to deal with it logically. However, if it's something you've expected or prepared for you will know what to do. This is one of the reasons that First Aid training is so important. When someone is hurt is not the time to learn what to do, it's a time for action and time is critical.

2. Why do you think that after all the time that Laren has had his c-com that it suddenly requests that he give it a name? The device is intelligent and can read his mind. It suspects that he will be more comfortable with it himself if it's more personalized. Furthermore, naming something is considered acceptance of responsibility in various cultures. Thus naming the c-com takes his relationship with

it to a different, more intimate level, allowing him to access more capabilities than previously.

3. What is karma? Why is it an appropriate name for the c-com? Karma is the principle that good and bad deeds will always be reciprocated. In other words, if you do good deeds, you will likewise be the beneficiary of goodness and if you do bad deeds, you will have misfortune of the same degree. It's an appropriate name for the c-com since it has the ability to execute Laren's commands which, if good, will bring benefit, and if bad, will bring misfortune.

Chapter 33 (Refractions)

1. What do you do when you have a big problem? Do you want to be alone or do you prefer to talk it over with someone you trust? Do you address it with your heart or head?

2. They say that pessimists are more realistic but optimists accomplish more. Which one are you? Do you always see the bright side of a situation or are you inclined to lean toward gloom and doom whenever anything goes wrong? Do you ever overreact? One way to gauge the importance of a problem is to consider whether in a day, week, month or year it will matter anymore. How can you improve how you deal with problems and challenges?

3. Can you sense other people's feelings? Those who can feel other's emotions are called empaths, which can be challenging because you can't always tell whether they're your feelings or someone else's. What are the pros and cons of such a sensitivity?

Chapter 34 (Results)

1. Have you ever had a dream that came true or other impression that made a difference in your life? What about your conscious dreams, what you want to happen or accomplish? Do you think that they'll come true just because you want them to or do you think you

have to take action and work for them? How would having a plan help?

2. Have you ever thought you'd solved a problem only to find out your solution wouldn't work? How did you handle the disappointment? Did you give up or try something else?

3. Have you ever been depressed? What did you do to overcome it? Did you turn to anyone for help? If you knew someone was depressed and considering ending their life what would you do?

Chapter 35 (Plans)

1. Who do you go to when you need advice or information? Do you go to someone who is knowledgeable or someone who will simply agree with you? It's always best when you have a question of a technical nature to talk to an expert. For example, if you were having trouble with your chemistry homework you wouldn't talk to your English teacher. The internet provides numerous options as well but make what you find is valid. Depending on what you're trying to research, the information it provides may not be accurate. How do you make sure it is?

2. What does the admonition "Question everything" mean to you? While it's nice to think that experts in a given subject know everything, this is not always the case. In many cases people do not deliberately lie, but have been given inaccurate information themselves. People at all levels make mistakes. How can you make sure that something is true?

3. Why would someone withhold the truth from others? It has been said that when you want to know the reason someone is lying or not providing important information that you should "follow the money." This means that it's likely that someone is profiting from lying. If that's the case, how can it help you to figure out the truth?

Chapter 36 (Preparations)

Why could it be dangerous for Karma to provide information without being asked? Sometimes people aren't ready, either emotionally, mentally or intellectually, to learn something which could cause harm to them or others.

Chapter 37 - 38 (Frozen Time and Finale)

1. Have you ever shared an intense or even traumatic experience with others? Such things as extreme weather and other natural disasters help people forget their differences and group together to survive. People who have served together in the military often develop close bonds and remain in touch their entire lives. On a less dramatic scale, academic sports teams can achieve a similar bond which lasts for years. Why do you think this occurs?

2. There are some goals that you can't achieve alone but require the help and support of others. Name some examples, such as becoming a famous actor.

Epilogue

What would the world be like if all negativity and hate were eliminated? What can you do as an individual to help create such a world?

* * *

The author would enjoy hearing about your experiences with these discussion & lesson plan suggestions. Feel free to contact her at marcha@kallioperisingpress.com.

If you're fascinated by science and want to learn more about physics, visit the author's blog at https://marcha2014.wordpress.com/category/physics-explained/

www.ingramcontent.com/pod-product-compliance
Lightning Source LLC
Chambersburg PA
CBHW071315130626
46556CB00004B/1618